West of the River, North of the Bridge

Stories from Michigan's U.P.

Richard Hill

Richard Hill

West of the River, North of the Bridge: Stories from Michigan's U.P.

By Richard Hill

Published by:

Gale Force Press

Sault Ste. Marie, Michigan

Editor: Tyler Tichelaar, Superior Book Productions

Cover and Interior Design: Stacey Willey, Globe Printing

Cover Photo of Crisp Point: Norris Seward

ISBN: 978-0-9817371-7-1

Library of Congress: 2020907211

First Printing 2020

Copyright © 2020 Richard Hill

Printed in the USA

Disclaimer: This is a work of fiction. All people, places, and events are the creation of the author's imagination or used fictitiously. Any similarity to live people or events is purely coincidental.

All Rights Reserved. No part of this book may be used or reproduced in any manner whatsoever without the expressed written consent of the author, except in the case of brief quotations with credit embodied in articles, books, and reviews.

Address all inquiries to:
Richard Hill, Gale Force Press
5480 W Cedar Drive, Sault Ste. Marie, MI 49783
906-632-8104, moosician@exede.net

To Judy, Travis, Coleman, and Max

Books by Richard Hill

Lake Effect: A Deckhand's Journey on the Great Lakes Freighters

Hitchhiking After Dark: Offbeat Stories from a Small Town

Lost in the Woods: Building a Life Up North

West of the River, North of the Bridge: Stories from Michigan's U.P.

Table of Contents

1

REBELLION

The River

In the summertime, the St. Mary's River teems with a multitude of whitefish, walleye, and salmon. Fishermen rise early to jockey their boats into position at their favorite spots up and down the river. The smaller boats have to keep a sharp lookout for any approaching freighters, many of them 600 to 1000 feet in length, giants that rule the Great Lakes waterway. These larger ships are unable to maneuver as rapidly as smaller vessels so they have to stay in the deeper shipping channel between buoys.

Every season, thousands of freighters hauling iron ore, coal, and grain traverse the St. Mary's through the Soo Locks, carrying their cargoes to ports across the world and around the Great Lakes. Cutting through the heart of Sault Ste. Marie, the Edison Sault Power Canal's waters, diverted from the river, churn through the turbines of the quarter-mile-long Union Carbide, providing power for the city and a harvest of flies and insects for the hungry trout and whitefish. By early July, the voracious fish are feeding in great numbers on the just-hatched mayflies and shad flies. Local fishermen tie their boats just behind the Carbide wall to fish in the swift currents and the deep water that joins the St. Mary's.

For the better part of the summer of 1967, Jake Powell and his younger brother, Jeremy, had fished behind the Carbide in their dad's fourteen-foot boat. It wasn't much to look at, but it was solid and reliable and had a twenty-horse Evinrude motor.

Though only fifteen and thirteen, the boys were entrusted with the boat and its safe operation. There was to be no joyriding or tomfoolery on the water, their dad had warned them. And life jackets were to be worn at all times. They got tired of hearing him say that, but they followed his orders.

Late one August, on a warm and humid evening, Jake and Jeremy set off on a short trip downriver to join some buddies who were throwing an end-of-summer cookout at Rotary Park, a small picnic area on the river, just across from Sugar Island. Since they had no access to a car, the boys got permission from their dad to take the boat. It was less than two miles by water, and they figured they could take a few friends on a short river-cruise before dark.

As the boys motored down the river, Jake steering from the stern seat, they approached Mission Point. The shipping channel there narrows to just over a hundred yards, and the current picks up speed. Nearing Clyde's Drive-In on the mainland side, they noticed the lines of cars parked along the river, mostly tourists enjoying the balmy summer evening. Jeremy, seated in the bow, waved vigorously to them, and they waved back.

Then, suddenly, as they were passing the ferry dock, the boat began to shake and groan. When Jeremy looked back, Jake was struggling to hold the motor's steering handle. A high-pitched squeal rose from the water, and the entire boat shuddered intensely. The boat was moving rapidly downstream in the current, but the motor was apparently snagged on something beneath the surface. Within a matter of seconds, the twenty-horse motor snapped off the transom and disappeared into the choppy water. The momentum nearly pulled Jake into the river, forcing him to release his grip.

"Quick, Jeremy! Grab the oars!"

The motor-less boat drifted swiftly in the current. Jeremy seized the wooden oars and tried to mount them in the oar locks, but the one on the port side was missing.

"We're short an oar lock; we have to paddle," said Jeremy.

Fast approaching Rotary Park, the boys both stood up in the boat and safely paddled their way over to the shore. Still in a slight state of shock and disbelief, they stopped and stared at the motor's remains—a jagged metal clamp still screwed to the boat's transom. It was a minor miracle that the force of the impact, whatever had caused it, hadn't broken off the entire transom mid-river. They would have lost both the boat and the motor. For the first time, they were both relieved to have been wearing life jackets; the swift current could have swept them under. Something beneath the water's surface must have snagged their propeller–a sunken cable or wire? They could not be sure. With all the shipping traffic passing through that particular point, it seemed an unlikely place to find an underwater obstruction.

At the cookout, Jeremy and Jake tried to make the best of the situation. While they downed a few brats and hamburgers, the boys tried to figure out what to do next. Several friends offered them a ride home, but the boys weren't sure about leaving their dad's boat at the park. Without a lock, it could easily be stolen.

As twilight settled in, the skies glowed with a rosy farewell, and the river's surface smoothed out and darkened. The last of the fishermen and their boats headed back to their docks to tie up for the night. A flock of honking Canada geese paraded in V-formations overhead as evening serenity settled over the river.

The picnic gear and food was soon packed away and disappeared with their friends. Jake and Jeremy stood by the river, staring at their injured boat, wondering how they could maneuver it up the darkening river.

"Let's just call Dad," said Jeremy. "We can find a phone over at Clyde's. Just call him and tell him what happened."

"There is no possible way we're doing that," Jake replied. "He won't understand that we just lost his twenty-horse motor. He's going to be so pissed. The least we can do is get the boat back to the dock."

"That oar lock is missing. How are we supposed to row the boat all the way up the river?" Jeremy asked.

Jake thought about that for a moment, then said, "Trust me. I've got a plan."

"If we call Dad, the worst would be that we'd be grounded for a long time," said Jeremy. "We can save a few bucks and buy him another motor. It wasn't even our fault."

"I don't want to get my ass kicked," Jake replied. "Maybe you do. C'mon; let's go. It's getting darker."

Jeremy was reluctant to follow his older brother's plan, but he finally decided to give it a shot. They had about twenty-five feet of line from the boat anchor that they tied to the nose of the bow. On the other end, they tied a loop for a hand-hold. Walking along the rocky bank, the boys slowly guided the boat up the river. It meandered from side to side in the strong river current. Since the Sugar Island ferry was briefly tied up on the island side, they were able to maneuver safely past the ferry dock without interference.

Making their way in the dark, Jeremy and Jake took turns hauling the boat line. While one pulled, the other stood in the boat and paddled like a gondolier. They climbed around several chain-link fences that marked private property on the shoreline. When they approached a large boat slip and marina, the only way past was to wade chest-deep in the river and pull.

Tugging the boat along, Jeremy was exhausted but didn't complain. Then, as he struggled against the current, the water became neck-deep. Even though it was late summer, the chill of the river water took his breath away.

"I can't pull anymore, Jake; it's over my head."

"Pull me over by the rocks and climb in. We'll have to paddle the rest of the way."

A full moon had risen over the river, reflecting off the black water. Lights from the Canadian side twinkled dimly from the distant north shore. Red and green channel buoys blinked in the night, marking the navigation limits. The boys' boat did not have any running lights as required by the Coast Guard. Except for their silhouettes in the moonlight, they were virtually invisible.

After Jeremy climbed aboard, the two of them stood up and paddled with the long wooden oars. They made slow progress against the stiff current and lost ground whenever they stopped to rest for a moment.

"I don't know," Jeremy said. "I just don't feel good about this. How are we ever going to paddle past the Carbide? That current is pretty swift coming out of the canal."

"We've got to get this boat back to its dock," Jake insisted. "That's all there is to it. Are you going to wimp out on me now?"

Jeremy was quiet for a while. He thought back to earlier in the summer when Jake had backed their dad's car into a light pole at McDonald's. Then, a couple of weeks later, Jake had received a ticket for doing ninety on I-75. That had been the last straw. Their dad had taken away the car keys for the rest of the summer. Jake had said he just wanted to see what the old man's car could do. Now he had no wheels, no ride to get around.

The only trouble Jeremy had been in that summer was for stealing a couple of his dad's beers from the fridge and wrecking the lawn mower blade on a tree stump. He had been earning some pocket money by mowing neighborhood lawns when he ran over a large, hidden oak stump that popped up out of nowhere. His dad had raised holy hell with him for that, but he didn't force him to pay for the damage.

The boys could sense they were slowly driving their father nuts with one incident after another. He was drinking and swearing at them more than usual, and it was obvious things were taking their toll. Their mother, on the other hand, seemed to take things in stride.

"Oh, Ethan," she'd say to their father, "don't worry so much. Boys will be boys. They're bound to get into trouble now and then; it's all part of growing up. Now just relax a little and settle down."

But their father couldn't. As his blood pressure climbed, even little things began to set him off. Lost car keys or eyeglasses would send him on a tear. The boys grew fearful of him. They were afraid to ask him for anything—the car, the boat, advice. They didn't want to upset him more than he already was.

Near exhaustion, Jeremy stood quietly in the boat, paddling upriver in the darkness. He realized Jake was probably right. They had no choice but to get their dad's boat back to its original berth or face dire consequences. No point in pushing their already frazzled father over the edge. Maybe, Jeremy thought, they could locate another boat motor and mount it before their father noticed it was missing.

As their vessel approached the stronger current sweeping

through the Carbide turbines, the boys got carried farther out into the river. Drained from paddling for so long, they could barely hold their place in the river. When they glanced upriver toward the Soo Locks, the boys suddenly recognized the lights from a six-hundred-foot freighter bearing down on them. The ship was still a half-mile away but was closing fast.

The freighter had departed the MacArthur Lock only a few minutes earlier on its down-bound journey to South Chicago. On the freighter's bow, a watchman standing lookout spotted something unusual in the river ahead. Through his binoculars, he identified the dark silhouettes of two figures in the moonlight, paddling a rowboat. He saw no visible running lights and assumed they were in distress. The lookout grabbed his walkie-talkie and called the mate in the ship's pilot house. The captain flipped on the powerful overhead spotlights and searched the river ahead. As he quickly located the stricken boat in his ship's path, the captain blasted the steam whistle eight short toots, indicating immediate danger. The narrow channel prevented the ship from altering its course. The captain instantly signaled the engine room to reverse engines, hoping to slow the ship's momentum. In the downstream current, this maneuver would never stop the ship, but it might help check her speed. The captain then radioed the Coast Guard for an emergency rescue.

The freighter loomed closer to the boys paddling in the darkness. They could make out the green starboard-side light on the ship's bow and a string of yellow deck lights, not fifty yards ahead. They paddled their hearts out to escape the ship's path, but it was too late.

In the moonlit shadows, amid the frantic blowing of the freighter's steam whistle, the ship's bow plowed into the small, helpless boat, catapulting the boys into the river. The stricken vessel capsized and sank within a matter of seconds. Almost immediately, deck personnel on the freighter threw life rings into the water to assist the boys.

Jeremy and Jake were separated in the river's blackness and called to each other. "Jake! Jake! I'm over here! Swim out of the wake, away from the suction."

"I'm coming, Jeremy! I can't see a damn thing out here!"

Jeremy had heard rumors from friends that the powerful freighter propellers created a strong suction as they neared you and could draw you into the blades. The boys floated downstream in the current, trying desperately to swim away from the ship.

In the darkness, Jake swam toward his brother's voice and soon located him. "Are you all right, Jeremy?"

"I'm okay, but exhausted," Jeremy said, resting his head back on his life jacket, drifting swiftly in the current. They shivered in the cold river water, trying to conserve enough energy to swim for shore.

They swam hard toward the mainland but became separated again in the current. As the enormous freighter passed them, the spotlight from the pilot house played over the river as if to pinpoint the swimmers' location.

Within a few minutes, a Coast Guard cutter appeared. As the vessel approached, with bright spotlights blazing, a voice came over the loudspeaker. "This is the U.S. Coast Guard. We'll throw you some life rings. Grab ahold and we'll help you aboard."

As the ship neared, the Coast Guard saw one of the boys clinging to a large navigation buoy. They picked Jeremy up and continued to search for Jake. They found him downstream from the Sugar Island ferry, floating helplessly in his life jacket. He was exhausted but relieved that their grueling ordeal was finally over.

~ ~ ~

After a Coast Guard officer brought the weary boys home that evening, they had a long story to tell their parents. Once their father had heard the entire tale of their ordeal in the river, he realized how close they had come to drowning. For the first time they could remember, their father hugged Jake and Jeremy for a long moment without speaking. He looked them both in the eye and said, "I'm so thankful to have you boys here tonight, safe and sound. We'll worry about that motor another day."

When things finally settled down, the boys had gained a newfound respect for the river and its elusive strength. They no longer took so much for granted. It had been a long, eventful summer, and the boys were ready for the change of season. Somehow, they would try to make it all up to their father; they felt that was the least they could do. But for now, dry land and home never felt so good.

Fog Whistles

If you want to know the truth, I have no right whatsoever to be here; the odds were simply not in my favor. But sometimes you just catch a lucky break, whether you deserve it or not.

Without a doubt, I should have wound up in jail, or reform school, or if I were lucky, working at McDonald's or Burger King for the rest of my days. Just when my life was circling the drain, some funny things happened to me. I never had the best luck growing up anyway, not that I'm complaining. I know friends who had it much worse–drugs, drunken abusive fathers, living in shelters. My life hasn't yet sunk to that level, but it is certainly teetering closer and closer to the edge.

Let me back up about five years, around the mid-90s, when I was living up in Sault Ste. Marie, in Michigan's Upper Peninsula—we just call it the U.P.—and attending the local high school as a sixteen-year-old junior. I was not the easiest kid to get along with. My quick temper always got the best of me, triggered by some high-strung teacher or some smart-mouthed punk. Teachers would say, "Phil, stop talking and pay attention, or I'll write you up for detention after school." That didn't faze me; I was too bored by the whole scene.

I talked back to teachers constantly or swore blue streaks at them, so they threw me out of classes on a regular basis. That was OK by me, since I could hang out downtown for the rest of the day or go for long walks down by the river. My mom, Eleanor, couldn't care less where I was. She was too busy working her Walmart cashier's job and running around with an endless stream of loser boyfriends to worry about me. Not that she didn't care; she did. I know because she cooked dinner for the two of us every night and occasionally made breakfast, if she could wake up in time.

I was late for school much of the time and didn't even really want to be there. Some of the hotshot guys made a big deal out of the fact that I wore black clothes all the time. They thought I must be a Goth or some devil worshipper just because I wore black T-shirts, black jeans, and a black coat. So far from the truth. I don't even have tattoos of any kind–they creep me out. Anyway, I just ignored them as long as I could. But the harassment was non-stop, so I pounced on one of them, punched him in the face, and even managed to break his nose.

I was transferred to the alternative high school on the other side of town. I continued to wear black every day, my favorite color, but no one hassled me about it. The other students seemed to have their own share of problems to deal with. With hair dyed orange, pink, and green and sporting tattoos and nose rings, this happy group of campers all had attitudes to match. They didn't want anyone telling them what to do or how to do it. We were all just a ragtag bunch of misfits, and we knew it. I seemed to fit right in.

It was a totally different atmosphere from regular high school, very casual, very loose. Everyone seemed to break off into their usual cliques of two or three students, which left me by myself. That was fine by me since I didn't know many others. Every couple hours, the teachers let us go outside for a smoke, which was cool. We tried not to swear in class, but when we accidently did swear, the teachers didn't blow a gasket or send us down to the principal's office. They kept their cool, and I respected that. The rules police weren't near as rigid as in my old school. Things here were loose and chill, a welcome change of pace for me.

Most teachers were still sticklers for finishing your homework and turning it in on time. I tried harder and got most of my work done. But something here was different. It was like the teachers were really pulling for each and every student, encouraging each one of us to read more, work harder, and think more clearly. They seemed to have more patience than we were used to and to tolerate more of the BS some students dished out. They didn't have that Gestapo mentality and thin skin like some of my old teachers. I started looking forward to attending classes every morning.

My mom works the afternoon shift at Walmart as a cashier. She can't take many days off, or she says they'll write her up and maybe let her go. Until she finds a better-paying job, she'll stick with this one. After work, Mom picks up groceries and comes home to make dinner. There's just the two of us.

I was kind of an unexpected visitor, according to Mom. She didn't even know she was pregnant for the longest time. My dad, Eddie to his friends, drove a pulpwood semi-truck back and forth across the U.P. He dated Mom for a few months but wouldn't marry her—said he didn't really want to settle down just yet. So, now that I'm nearly grown, he comes over to the house some nights to watch TV, when he's in town, with a six-pack of Bud under his arm and a Little Caesar's pizza. I barely know him. He's been gone most of my life and is trying, in kind of a half-hearted way, to make up for it. I think of him as a long lost, visiting uncle. Mom doesn't hate him, but she's not exactly nuts about him either. With a new boyfriend every other month or so, she keeps up a busy social calendar. So she's not quite holding her breath, thinking Eddie could be the man of her dreams, but she likes the company. Over the years, he's apparently given her too many nightmares. Eddie used to come home half-drunk, carrying on 'til all hours of the night. He would pound on her locked bedroom door, trying to get in. I never saw him hit her, but his all-night yelling sprees scared the bejesus out of both of us, until he fell asleep. The next morning, he acted like nothing had ever happened. Nevertheless, like a stray dog, he keeps showing up, looking for another bone to chew.

Maybe that's the one thing I inherited from my dad–the ability to keep showing up, even when it doesn't make total sense. At the old high school, I was usually bored, angry, and rebellious at everything, for no particular reason. I simply couldn't connect with anybody or any of the material they were teaching. I kept wondering, *What good will this do me?* Nothing made any clear sense to me. Dudes drifting through the hallways would say, "Phil, are you lost in the cosmos to-day, or did you forget your meds?" They'd laugh and walk on down the hallway, pointing back at me like I'm some kind of moron. I would simply go into my expressionless dead zone and tune them out completely. It was my protection from all the noise and chaos.

Attending alt-school was like discovering an island in white-water rapids, a welcome pause that helps you catch your breath. I wasn't really expecting much when I came here, so this difference caught me off guard. One day in English class, Ms. Edwards happened to stop by my desk when she was handing out graded papers. She glanced down at my notebook and noticed my pencil sketches and doodles. I had sketched some freighters on the river and some boats in the harbor.

"Phil," she said, "those are some really excellent sketches. You're quite good at that."

"Oh, thanks," I said. "I was just messing around." No one,

not even my mom or dad, had ever said a good word about any of my doodles. I drew pictures just to keep from getting bored.

"Maybe you have a hidden talent for art," Ms. Edwards said. "Keep it up. I'd like to see more of your work sometime." She smiled at me and handed out the remaining papers.

I suddenly felt awakened, not all at once, but like I was coming out of a deep sleep. Something long dormant had crept back into my consciousness. I wasn't used to receiving compliments from anyone, for anything, so it was a little confusing. I didn't quite know how to deal with it. But if there were ever such a thing as a spark of inspiration, this must have been it.

Over the next several weeks, Ms. Edwards did something unusually kind for me. She pulled me aside after class one day and gave me a sketchbook for my drawings. She told me to sketch anything that interested me–trees, boats, people, still lifes.

A week later, she dropped off a box of drawing pencils with different lead densities. Then it was a set of charcoal sticks, which were very messy at first, but soon opened up a whole new world for me.

Before long, Ms. Edwards approached the regular art teacher from my old high school and arranged for me to attend a drawing class there once a week. I was a little leery about mixing it up again with some of those students who had bullied me at the old high school, but I didn't seem to have any real issues. At least not at first.

In art class, we studied perspective, gesture drawing, gradients, shading, and even worked with a couple of live models. I was completely focused and absorbed in everything about the class. *Why hadn't anybody exposed me to this before?* I wondered. Counselors had always steered me toward welding and shop classes–nothing like this. Drawing was such a no-brainer for me. The class also offered me a chance to paint with watercolors and oils—not at all an easy thing to learn.

One day, after a couple of months of art classes, some smart-assed kid named Kevin walked up to me before class and started snickering under his breath. He was checking out some of my charcoal sketches and said, "You call this art? You can't draw worth a shit."

"Get lost," I said, and tried to ignore him.

"No, seriously, dude. My dog could do a better job. This is nothing but crap."

"I don't need your opinion, slimeball," I said. "Go crawl back in your hole."

But the guy wouldn't leave me alone. "Why are you wasting your time? You really suck, man."

Something snapped inside me, and I wheeled around and punched him in the face. I really couldn't help myself. I think I loosened a couple of his teeth and may have broken his nose. He was bleeding all over when the teacher pulled us apart. She sent me to the principal's office and Kevin to the school nurse. I was kicked out of my art class for good and permanently sent back to alt-school.

The whole episode upset me so much and seemed so unfair that I burned off some of my anger by channeling it into my drawings. My images became more intense and emotional, the colors more vibrant and explosive. For some reason, I wanted to draw abstract pictures of wrecked cars, burned-out houses, and ship collisions in the river. It was as if I were communicating something without spelling it out in detail, suggesting something without being too literal.

When I finished these pieces, I felt like I'd run a marathon;

I was exhausted, but satisfied with my effort. I had finally expressed something in myself that had lain hidden for so long, and it felt amazing.

My classes at the alt-school were seldom boring. Despite the less strict rules, some students still tried to rebel or take advantage of a teacher's kindness. Sometimes in the middle of class, a couple of students would grow a bit restless and climb out the first-floor window to have a smoke. That riled up the teacher enough to send them to the office, if she could even locate them outside. Other students would sometimes put their feet up on the desk in front of them and try to take a snooze. The teacher would quietly walk over to the snoozer and shake a cowbell in their ear. That usually rattled the student's cage enough to keep them awake the rest of the morning.

One afternoon, in Ms. Edwards' English class, she was listing some figures of speech on the blackboard. In the back of the room, Tony, Karl, and Marsha were busy whispering back and forth, totally ignoring the teacher up front. After repeated attempts to quiet them, Ms. Edwards turned around, gave them a long blank stare, and finally said, "Listen, guys; if you don't want to be delivering pizza for the rest of your lives, you need to start paying attention."

That stopped them in their tracks. For the first time I could remember, they were totally speechless–no excuses, no smart-ass remarks. The three of them blushed with embarrassment. Then Tony stood up and said:

"We don't have to listen to that kind of crap." And he stomped out of the classroom, followed closely by Karl and Marsha. I heard that they headed straight for the principal's office and complained that they were grossly insulted by Ms. Edwards' comment. They had their pride, and it had been wounded.

But a strange thing happened not long afterwards. When the three students returned to class a few days later, they seemed to be paying closer attention and tackled their homework more diligently. Something had unwittingly shaken their comfortable world like a cold slap in the face. I'm sure Ms. Edwards wasn't trying to be rude to them; she's not like that. And it was surely no slam on the pizza industry; I think she was just trying to get their attention, and that's how it came out.

~ ~ ~

On foggy days, usually in early spring or fall, the giant lake freighters that ply the St. Mary's River help prevent collisions by blowing their steam whistles every few minutes to alert other ships of their relative positions. As students, we often tend to navigate in a perpetual haze, vaguely aware of distant fog whistles warning us to stay alert. For the most part, we ignore them and wind up paying a price. But, as with everything, our navigation skills improve with age and experience.

As the school year wore on, I focused on my portfolio more seriously. Portraits of people became my specialty. I drew a sketch of my mother in her bathrobe, watching TV game shows with a cup of coffee. Then I sketched a portrait of my father standing proudly alongside his big-rig, silver semi-tractor. My folks didn't seem at all impressed. Maybe they thought drawing was a frivolous waste of time, but I thought I was making some serious progress.

In the spring, Ms. Edwards insisted I enter an art show up at Lake Superior State University (LSSU), the local college. It was an open competition for high school students in the U.P. I entered a charcoal self-portrait that I had recently completed, and it won first place for my age category. I was completely blown away; I had never won anything in my life.

LSSU was hosting an awards dinner to celebrate all of the

artists, but when the time arrived, my mother was too tired and hung over to attend. It was on the weekend, and she had been out partying the night before. I didn't really want to go to the dinner by myself and was just going to skip it. Then, on a lark, I called up Ms. Edwards and asked her to fill in. She didn't hesitate for a moment.

The awards dinner was amazing—all these talented high school artists from across the entire U.P. in one room. When I looked around the banquet room at the wide variety of drawings and other pieces of art, I was stunned to see all these people paying so much attention to art. To artists themselves. I had no idea. It was a world that, not long ago, I was oblivious to. Now, in a small way, I was a part of it. When my name was announced, everyone applauded and I walked up to the podium to receive a framed first-place certificate. Ms. Edwards beamed at me and shook my hand, saying, "Philip, I hope you take your talent seriously and go as far as you can. I am so proud of you." I choked up a little and simply nodded that I would.

My senior year flew by in a blur of activity, and soon enough, graduation was approaching. With encouragement from Ms. Edwards and one of my counselors, I applied to several art schools around Michigan. In late May, my counselor called me down to his office and handed me a letter from Kendall College of Art and Design in Grand Rapids. I had been accepted for the fall term and awarded a full scholarship to attend. My head was spinning, I was so excited. Art school? Me? And Kendall, of all places? It was one of the best art schools in Michigan and had a stellar reputation in the art world.

When I arrived home to announce the news to my mother, I saw a note on the kitchen table:

Dear Philip,

I've decided to head out west to California with my boyfriend Ralph to try my luck. It couldn't be any worse than around here. I'm sick of my Walmart job and figure I'd better get out of town to try something new while I've still got the nerve. I heard the jobs out there pay a heckuva lot better. Wish me luck.

Hope you find some kind of work this summer. Make the best of it–nothing's ever easy. Don't I know. I'll try to send you a few bucks when I can.

Love, Eleanor (Mom)

I carefully folded my acceptance letter, slipped it into my back pocket, and stepped out the door for a long walk. From then on, I knew I was on my own, nobody to look after me. I wished I had more friends to lean on right then, but I didn't.

I walked for miles around town that night, then wandered down by the river and sat on the bank. It was a cool evening in May, and a dense fog was settling over the ships in the river. I could barely make out the running lights and the pilot house of a passing freighter as it drifted by me in a ghostlike mirage, its powerful engine thumping rhythmically in the darkness. Farther down the river, I heard a muted fog whistle from a distant freighter. I sensed the hidden shoals ahead and the uncertain course I would have to navigate by myself. It was a lonely, chilling feeling, but all in all, it felt good to be striking out on my own.

In the coming months, I would have to find a summer job and apply for financial aid at Kendall. And to share expenses and make ends meet, I would probably have to find a roommate for the short term. This opportunity was not going to slip away from me.

~ ~ ~

That was all several years ago, and things for me have changed since then. It's quite a challenge here at art school, but I'm making the most of my good fortune–I'm well aware of the alternatives. I'll never figure out what I ever did to win the lottery. What are the odds for someone like me? Probably not so good.

Early on in my life, the world always looked unfriendly to me; I would have to fight for everything and struggle to survive. And I was partly right. But I never appreciated until now the fact that there are kind and concerned people in the world like Ms. Edwards and others who come along and show you a different perspective. I needed that. And I'm so thankful.

For certain, the world doesn't look quite the same to me anymore. The closer I look at things, the more I see. Perception goes way beyond the first glance.

The Education of Louie Salastino

Living on a bricklayer's wages, Louie Salastino and his wife, Grace, had raised two boys, Tony and Joe. Louie taught them about discipline and hard work, about making good choices and trying to do the right thing. For the most part, they were good boys who listened to their father. Both boys came of age in the late 1960s, a time when young men could still be drafted into the Army and go to war–just as Louie had done some twenty-five years earlier. When Uncle Sam drafted him, Louie Salastino had proudly served his country, and now he expected his boys, if called upon, to do their duty. He wasn't prepared for what happened.

Louie's oldest son, Tony, was a remarkable athlete. At six-foot three, he could drive the length of the court and slam-dunk the ball before the other team could move a muscle. Tony was tall and slender, but he could run like the wind. He played starting guard on his high school varsity team, and during his senior year, he hoped to catch the eye of a recruiter from one of the Michigan college teams, even though academics was not his strong suit. Tony wasn't really interested in hitting the books—he just wanted to keep on playing hoops. A scholarship to play basketball and possibly a free ride to college would be a dream come true.

Louie and Grace went to all of Tony's games. For Friday night games, Louie prepared a special pasta and meat-sauce dish; it gave his son extra strength in the closing minutes of the game, when everything was on the line. They came early to the games to get a good seat and yell encouragement to Tony from the stands. They tried not to badger the refs, but sometimes they couldn't resist. The refs made their share of bad calls, and Tony's parents were there to keep them honest.

The war was on, and many of Tony's former teammates had been drafted into the army and sent to Vietnam. Some had returned without a scratch; a few others had shrapnel wounds or were missing limbs.

Tony was upset with the war and what it had done to his friends. His dad had served in the army during World War II, stationed first in France, then in Italy, fighting to stop Hitler from taking over the world. But, to Tony, Vietnam was not the same kind of war. It was more of a standoff of unintelligible chaos and unrealistic goals. After being bogged down for several years, Americans couldn't agree on whether to stay and fight or cut their losses and leave.

Tony's younger brother, Joseph, was a junior in high school and didn't have to worry about the draft yet. He was not an athlete like his brother, but he liked to hunt and fish, especially during trout season when he could head off into the woods to cast a line on a quiet stream. Joe reveled in the peaceful woods of the U.P.'s Pine River and Sullivan Creek near Raco. He loved the solitude of the darkened woods and the way you could quietly approach a stream and cast a hand-tied fly into a deep shady hole. It relaxed him and made him forget the rest of the world for a while.

By the time graduation rolled around, Tony had not heard from a single recruiter and had not been offered any scholarships to play ball. He thought it may have been because of the time he was caught smoking marijuana on the bus during an away trip downstate. His coach had suspended him for a game, and maybe the story had leaked out. He couldn't be sure. One thing was certain—he wouldn't be playing hoops for any school that fall.

When summer came, Tony joined a couple of buddies and drove out to Boston to find work. The war was turning uglier, and his draft number would be coming up in the fall. He did not want to think about it, but he did not want to be sent to Vietnam either. Between talking to his friends and seeing the stories on TV and in the papers, Tony was quickly choosing sides.

Vicious anti-war protests had filled Boston's downtown streets for months. Students versus police, tear gas, billy clubs, cars set on fire. Tony didn't understand the politics involved—who did?—nor the need to take sides. He was hoping the war would soon come to an end, and then things would calm down. But there was great fear and uncertainty in the air.

Tony felt an obligation to serve his country in some way, as his friends and former classmates had done, but he did not want to take part in a war he saw as pointless and out of control. It seemed like a mindless meat grinder with no clear justification.

When October arrived, Tony's draft number came up, and he was ordered by the U.S. government to report for induction. His father called from Michigan to see what his son had decided.

"I'm being drafted into the army, Dad. They want me to report for service next month."

"I'm proud of you, son. The army will do you some good. There's no point in drifting around in circles like a lost hippie. I fought for this country for three years in World War II, and it's your duty to do the same."

"Well," Tony hesitated, "I'm not quite sure what I should do."

"What do you mean?" Louie asked.

"This war is not the same as the one you fought in, Dad. The papers I've been reading say this is a civil war and maybe the U.S. made a big mistake by getting involved."

"Listen, son, when your country asks you to serve, you need to step up. I raised you to do what's right. I know it's tough, but it's your patriotic duty!"

There was a long pause, and then Tony said, "I need more time to think about it."

That fall, Tony did not report for induction as instructed by the government. He had found a part-time job as a carpenter's helper, nailing and framing walls as needed and cleaning up the construction site. Along with several draft-resisting friends, he had rented a third-floor apartment in a poorer part of town.

The antiwar protests and rallies had heated up over the winter months and seemed to embolden many of the long-haired students. By April, they were marching throughout the Boston Commons where speeches were given by returning army and marine veterans. The former soldiers rallied the crowd by recalling bloody stories of worthless sacrifice in jungles halfway around the world. Some took medals of honor they had earned and pitched them spitefully into a nearby bonfire. The crowd cheered wildly.

Before the police arrived to break up the unlawful protest, a handful of students had lit their draft cards near the blazing bonfire and held the burning embers aloft, chanting, "Hell, no, we won't go! Hell, no, we won't go!" Again the crowd responded approvingly, shouting, "End the war! End the war!"

Tony reached into his wallet, found his draft card, and hurled it into the fire. Local TV cameras recorded the raucous scene for the evening news. Journalists with microphones interviewed nearby students to get their side of the story, but Tony wanted no part of it. He felt driven, but he was not proud of what he had done. He had crossed the line and realized that now there was no turning back.

When he had moved to his apartment, Tony had not given his family or friends back home any forwarding address. He feared the government or local police might trace his mail and throw him in jail for draft evasion. He knew he was walking a dangerous path and it was just a matter of time before he stumbled.

One evening in early summer, having showered after a long, hot day's work, Tony heard the door open suddenly. It was one of his roommates, Gary.

"Tony, there's two state police officers coming in the front door. I think they're coming for you."

In a panic, not wanting to hang around to answer questions, Tony grabbed his coat and some cash from his dresser drawer, crawled out the third-floor window to the fire escape, and vanished into the night. Jail was his very last option; anything else was better.

Within a few weeks, he had hitchhiked to Buffalo and crossed into Canada. He worked his way over to Toronto, where he had heard there was a collective of American draft resisters. Now he would have to figure out his life one day at a time. To avoid arrest, he knew there would be no returning to the States.

~ ~ ~

When Joe graduated from high school that spring, he was

not mentally prepared for college in the fall. He was a good student with decent grades, but he needed time off to decide on a career direction. Going to college someday was a goal of his, but not just because his buddies were going, many simply to avoid the draft. In the meantime, Joe became eligible for the draft and, soon enough, he received a letter instructing him to report for service that fall.

His brother Tony, in Canada, had sent him several letters espousing his antiwar views, trying to convince Joe to resist the draft. Tony never left a return address on the envelope for fear of being traced back to his location. So, as much as he wanted to, Joe could not respond.

A week before his induction, Joe packed up his fishing rod, a few beers, and some food, and without telling anyone, headed out to the family hunting cabin in the woods near Raco. It was only a half-hour's drive from home. No one would bother him out there.

For several days, Joe fished on Sullivan Creek and other nearby streams, trying to sort out his options. The maples and oaks had turned to scarlet and started to drop their leaves. The nights were getting cool enough that he had to fire up the pot-belly woodstove to warm up the cabin. For dinner, he caught several speckled trout and fried them up in a cast iron skillet. He loved the solitude of the woods–no radio or TV, no other voices to disturb him, just the melodies of songbirds in the morning and the rustle of wind in the night.

But a barrage of questions bombarded him in his sleep, and he tried to sort them out. *Why,* Joe wondered, *would I want to give all this up to fight in the jungles of Southeast Asia? What sort of fate awaits me in Vietnam? Will I come home in a body bag?* His friends were boldly volunteering for duty; some were being drafted. Certainly it would be a grand adventure, a chance to break away from the monotony of small-town life.

For a while, he daydreamed about driving his Ford pickup across the rural Upper Peninsula to stay out of the army. They'd never be able to track him through the woods and rural villages. He could work odd jobs for cash, fish the streams, and keep moving. But how long before that became tiresome? Before winter moved in?

Joe had been holed up in the cabin by himself four or five nights when a car suddenly drove up. It was his father.

"Thought I might find you out here, Joe," Louie said, walking in the door.

"I needed some time to think. It's all happening way too fast. Everything's so quiet and peaceful out here; I hate to give it all up."

"This place, humble as it is, will still be here when you return, son. It's not going anywhere."

Joe poked the embers in the woodstove and tossed in another log. "I'm afraid . . . afraid of going away and never seeing you and Mom and Tony again."

"Listen, son; we feel the same way about you, but you've just got to block that out of your mind. It'll eat you up." Louie reached for a beer in the cooler and cracked it open. "Speaking of Tony, your mom and I just received a letter from him. He's hiding out somewhere up in Canada, I'm not sure where, waiting for the war to blow over. I don't know what's come over him lately."

"Well, that's his choice," Joe replied, "and he'll have to live with the consequences. I sure miss him, though."

Louie crossed the room, put his arm around Joe's shoulders, and said, "Son, you've had all week here to mull things over, and you're due to report within two days. Are you going?"

Joe stared out the window at a deer that had just wandered into the clearing by the cedar trees. "Yeah, I'm going."

~ ~ ~

Within days, Joe boarded a Greyhound bus and reported to boot camp in South Carolina. By December, his company had received orders that it was shipping out for DaNang, where it would begin its one year of combat duty. Joe wrote home as often as he could, describing some of the bloody battles he was in, the casualties, the insufferable jungle heat, and the mosquitoes, counting the days until he could leave.

Down at the American Legion, where Louie occasionally stopped for a few beers after work, there was nonstop talk about how the war in Nam was going. He was proud to brag about Joe over in DaNang serving his country and sticking it to the enemy. But when some of the veterans asked him about Tony, he said he hadn't heard much from him lately. Louie felt too embarrassed to say that his son was a draft resister who had burned his card and that he'd fled to somewhere up in Canada. The vets would never stomach that kind of talk. There would be too much explaining to do. Only a couple of years earlier, he had been so proud of Tony, the basketball star of his hometown. It was such an honor to be his father. Everywhere he went, he had felt like such a celebrity. Those days were long gone now. Times had changed. His sons were now grown men with decisions of their own to make.

~ ~ ~

In June of 1971, *The New York Times* published part of the Pentagon Papers, a confidential government report on political and military involvement in Vietnam over the last twenty-five years. As it turned out, the United States had known for many years that the war was unwinnable, that the best-case scenario the country could expect was a stalemate. According to this top secret report, the number-one reason the U.S. stayed in Vietnam was to avoid a humiliating defeat. And yet, massive amounts of blood and money had continued to pour into the war effort so the U.S. could save face. Countless lives were sacrificed to avoid political embarrassment. And the public was told none of this. They were deceived by their government and led to believe the U.S. could win this war in the end if the American people were strong and persistent.

~ ~ ~

When Louie heard the news and finally digested it, he was disgusted with the American government. The Pentagon Papers report had been front page news across the country. For months, Walter Cronkite had reported more follow-up stories on *The CBS Evening News*. Louie had ignored these stories for a long period, thinking they were just more antiwar rhetoric trying to undermine the country. Then the more closely he followed the news on TV and in the papers, the more it began to make sense: the government had been deceiving the American public for many years about the war but had not altered its course. U.S. honor, sacrificing for one's country—all to protect us from national humiliation and embarrassment. These official justifications were all starting to sound so hollow and meaningless to him. The chess game had ended years earlier, but the government hadn't been willing to admit it.

When Louie thought of Joe, stationed in DaNang, he felt like the war was being conducted under false pretenses. He had not been told the truth—nobody had. So many American lives had been sacrificed. So many thousands had been wounded—needlessly—cavalierly—thoughtlessly. Louie began to worry more about his son's life in Vietnam. Would it be cut short? And for no good reason?

One evening, the phone rang. It was Tony, calling from Canada. "Dad, I've been thinking for a long time about things you said, about how you served your country when you were my age."

"Well, son," he interrupted, "I've said some angry things to you in the past about avoiding the draft and serving your country, but in the long run, maybe you were right."

"What . . . ? What do you mean?"

"You were right to protest the war, right to resist the draft, right to question our involvement over there. All of that."

When Tony learned that his father had become well aware of the Pentagon Papers report, he was stunned. His father had always been patriotic toward his country, but now patriotism had taken on an entirely new meaning for him. It was fair to question the morals and scruples of one's country and still love and respect it. The two were still compatible.

"I don't quite know what to say, Dad," said Tony, fighting back tears, "but . . . thank you. Thank you. I'm just so relieved to hear those words from you."

"I'm only sorry that it took so long to open my eyes. All along, we thought this war was a slam dunk. No such thing, as it turns out."

"Yeah, slam dunks used to be easy for me, too . . . but not anymore. For now, I'm thinking about getting into college and eventually joining the Peace Corps. I still want to help this country out in some way, if I can."

"That's great, son. I trust your judgment. I knew you'd figure things out eventually."

~ ~ ~

With a month left to serve in Vietnam, Joe stepped on a

land mine while on night patrol in the jungle and was instantly killed. His body was returned to his hometown, where he was buried with honors. His family was proud that he had served his country, but to his father, his son's sacrifice was hollow and pointless. Louie wanted to believe in honor and patriotism, but he found it very difficult. Heroes deserved so much more.

After work, Louie didn't hang around the American Legion much anymore. Too many vets supported the war, at any cost. Maybe it was easier for them to wave the flag than to question the meaning of patriotism. When he did occasionally stop at the Legion, he played pool or a few games of cribbage with his old friends. To keep the peace, he avoided political discussion entirely and stuck mainly to talk about the struggling Tigers and Lions. Old friends were still dear friends—no point in rattling those brittle bones.

Scout's Honor

Jake Powell and Chaz had been good friends throughout grade school. They loved summer camping in the woods and had both joined the Boy Scouts, Troop #107, several years earlier. When they each turned sixteen that summer, their attention was suddenly side-tracked by the appearance of so many good-looking high school girls. Until then, the boys had never quite noticed the magnetic attraction and hypnotic spell certain girls could put them under. On special scouting days, both boys felt self-conscious wearing their scout uniforms to school; this was encouraged but not required. They hadn't minded the uniforms in middle school, but high school was a very different matter. Amid many jibes and snickers from other students, they stuck with it because they still enjoyed all the outdoor scouting activities and camaraderie. At other times, they considered dropping out of the troop completely.

Their week-long summer camp, up near Munising, had come and gone that July of 1968. They both had a blast camping in pup tents, cooking over a campfire, swimming, canoeing, and hiking with the rest of their troop. The fierce mosquito population was another story, but by far, the best parts were the ghost stories around the campfire every evening.

When mid-August arrived, they realized only two weeks of summer vacation were left before school started. For Jake, it was a perennial thing, the feeling he had to cram three months' worth of summer vacation into the last few days of

August. One last kick. Sometimes, his ideas backfired—like the previous summer when he and his younger brother Jeremy had borrowed their father's fourteen-foot boat and somehow busted off the motor in the St. Mary's River. This getaway would be different—simply camping and hanging out together.

Along with their friend Wally, who was a year younger, Jake and Chaz headed out to camp at a friend's cabin near Raco, a small settlement twenty-some miles west of the Soo that had been a CCC camp during the Depression. This would be their last fling before hitting the books again that fall.

Jake, having earned the rank of Star, was the senior patrol leader and, along with the scoutmaster, was in charge of running most of the troop's activities. Chaz had risen to the rank of First Class and earned merit badges in cycling, coin collecting, and hiking. His parents were very proud of him and encouraged his ambition. Wally, whose parents were divorced, had joined Scouts a year earlier, but had worked his way up quickly and recently received his First Class badge as well. He was a hard, conscientious worker, always worried about doing the right thing.

Instead of tent-camping, the boys slept in the small rustic cabin and cooked their meals over a firepit outside. There was no electricity on the property and only an outhouse for the necessities. At night, they would need the light of two kerosene lanterns to find their way around the camp.

On Friday afternoon, Jake's dad had driven them out to the cabin and dropped them off for the weekend. To keep their eggs, sausage, and stew meat fresh, they had brought along a Coleman cooler filled with ice. The older cooler belonged to Wally and had several cracks in the bottom from overuse, so they left the cooler outside the door where it could slowly drain on the ground. It also made a little more room inside the cramped cabin.

Once they had their gear stowed in the cabin, the boys hiked through the woods to the fire tower several miles away. The mosquitoes, which had been ravenous earlier in the summer, were now few and far between. From the tower's peak, they took in a kaleidoscopic view of the North Woods just as the fall colors were hinting of change. They noticed very few cabins in the thousands of acres of wilderness before them.

By the time they returned to camp, the boys were hungry for dinner. Chaz gathered the firewood for cooking while Wally prepared the hamburgers and beans. After dinner, until almost midnight, they played rummy and penny ante poker and told stories before drifting off to sleep.

The boys slept until nine the next morning, and Jake was the first one out the door to pee. A second later, he exclaimed, "Oh, no! Guys, come here quick!"

Chaz and Wally raced out the door and took a look around. "We've been had! Look at this place. Must have been a bear here last night, though I didn't hear a thing."

From the cabin to the firepit, eggshells and meat wrappers were scattered. Milk cartons were flattened and cottage cheese containers emptied. An animal, most likely a bear, had wiped out their food supply in the cooler outside.

"Well," Jake said, "no stew tonight, boys. We're down to canned beans and tuna. Should've never left the fresh food out there. So much for that leaky cooler."

They cleaned up the mess and scraped together what they could for breakfast. By late morning, the boys hiked a few miles down the road to the fish hatchery and inspected thousands of tiny rainbow trout that would soon be planted in local lakes and streams. They tried their luck fishing at a beaver pond back in the woods but had no action. Too hot in the afternoon, they figured, for any fish to bite.

Early that evening, after a meager dinner, the boys grew restless and decided to take a hike through the woods. They came upon another cabin about half a mile away whose windows were dark, with the curtains drawn. Clearly, no one was home. Chaz noticed an antenna on the roof and suggested they try to get in to watch a little TV. Wally was the first to challenge him.

"You want to break into someone else's cabin and watch their TV? Are you nuts?"

"Don't get excited, little man," said Chaz. "We won't disturb anything. What harm is there?"

They checked several of the double-hung windows and found one that was unlocked. Jake slid in head first and unlocked the door for the others. They clicked on a couple of battery-powered lanterns sitting on a long, picnic-style table, then flipped on the 19-inch black-and-white TV. For nearly an hour, the boys watched an episode of *Gunsmoke*, captivated by the adventures of Matt Dillon and Miss Kitty. But Wally was getting nervous.

"OK, guys, we've got to clear out of here before someone comes. If anyone shows up, we would be so screwed."

"Yeah, maybe you're right," said Chaz.

They straightened up the chairs and the window curtains just as they had been. Jake opened one of the cabinet doors and noticed some canned vegetables and a box of instant Idaho potatoes. He loaded them up in his knapsack, then grabbed a stack of old *Life* magazines.

"We'll just borrow a few things for the night," he said. "We can return them tomorrow."

"Are you crazy?" said Wally. "If we get caught, we'll be thrown in jail. And we'll get kicked out of Scouts for sure!"

"Relax," said Jake, "We'll be all right."

Chaz found a six-pack of beer in a corner cabinet and grabbed a portable radio. "Maybe we can pull in a Tigers game tonight. C'mon; let's go."

Jake snatched up the other lantern and took one last look around in the back room. He suddenly froze. In the dim shadows of the lantern's light, he couldn't believe his eyes. Protruding from beneath the bunk beds, on the floor, was a woman's arm. A body beneath the bed had been wrapped in an army blanket, but a pale arm extended from the shadows. A diamond wedding ring sparkled on the finger of her left hand.

"Holy crap, guys! Come here. Quick!"

Chaz and Wally peered at the ghostly white arm and ran for the door.

"Let's get the hell out of here!" Wally yelled. "Before it's too late."

They raced back to their camp and tossed their knapsacks in the corner. Chaz was breathing hard and pacing the room. "Whose body could that possibly be? It doesn't look like she's been dead for very long. Should we call the cops?"

"Hold on," said Jake, cracking open one of the canned beers. "Let's think about this. If we call the cops, they'll know we broke into that cabin. Maybe the person who killed that woman and stuffed her under the bed will return soon to bury the body."

Wally started shaking and could barely speak. "Guys, let's just report the body and face the consequences," he said. "I don't want to stick around here."

"I don't think so," said Jake. "If the cops find out about the break-in, they might think we had something to do with the murder. We can't take the chance."

The boys stayed up until midnight arguing over what to do next and soon turned out the lights. But they couldn't sleep, worrying about whether someone might be stalking them.

"If someone breaks down our door looking for us," Chaz whispered in the dark, "we have no weapons to defend ourselves."

Wally leaped out of his sleeping bag and grabbed three long butcher knives from the kitchen drawer. Each boy slipped one under his pillow. Through the curtain, light from a full moon poured in. Off in the woods, a whippoorwill called, and a pack of coyotes began to howl softly in their nightly ritual. A warm wind rustled the pine boughs above the small cabin. The boys listened intently, their eyes focused on the locked door and windows, wondering if a killer lurked nearby in the woods.

When daylight arrived, the boys crawled out of their bunks and scraped together a makeshift breakfast from the canned Spam and beans they had pilfered from the other cabin. They clicked on the radio, hoping they might pick up some news or police reports about a murder, but all they could tune in to were Sunday morning church services and gospel hours. The fear and anxiety of the night before seemed to ease up in the bright morning sunshine. They washed the breakfast dishes and straightened up the camp, then burned their trash in the firepit outside.

Late that morning, a Michigan State Police car pulled up, and the officer knocked on the screen door. "Good morning, gentlemen. I'm Officer Matthews, and I'm out here this morning to have a look around at things. How long have you boys been camping out here?"

Jake stepped forward. "We've been here since Friday afternoon. We're scouts from Troop #107, just working on some of our merit badge requirements."

"Notice anything unusual the last couple of days or see anyone coming or going?" the officer asked.

"No," said Jake, "pretty quiet around here. We haven't seen or heard anyone since we got here, except for a black bear that stole our food a couple of nights ago."

"How 'bout you two?" the officer asked, looking at Chaz and Wally. They shook their heads.

"No, haven't seen a thing, officer."

The trooper peered through the screen door and said, "Mind if I come in and take a peek around?"

"Help yourself," Jake offered.

The officer walked slowly around the small room and picked up a few *Life* magazines. He noted the mailing address and name on them. He glanced at the portable radio and noted the brand. Then he saw the empty beer cans near the sink.

"Boys, a breaking-and-entering was reported this morning just a half-mile down the road. These are some of the missing items in your possession. I'm going to have to file a report."

The boys stared sheepishly down at the floor. They realized they had been caught red-handed. There was no point in trying to talk their way out of it. They gave the officer their names and addresses and told him they were due to be picked up by their parents later that afternoon.

"OK, gentlemen," the officer said. "I'll be contacting your parents today, and we'll see if the cabin owner wants to file charges against you."

The trooper pulled away in his patrol car, and the boys

stood there stunned. They had been too nervous to mention the body in the cabin's back room. They figured the murderer must have removed the body earlier that morning and buried it somewhere before calling the police about the break-in. But why would the killer want the police sniffing around there? It didn't make any sense.

"We've got to get away from here right away," said Chaz. "That guy will be tracking us down at any moment."

Wally hung his head and moaned. "Our parents will ground us for a year and make us quit Scouts. We are so screwed now."

The boys felt bad about the break-in and realized they had gone too far. *What kind of Scouts were they anyway?* they wondered—stealing from other people. There was no explanation for it other than teenagers looking for a little harmless excitement.

Jake sat at the table with his head in his hands. "That's right; we are toast. Let's pack up and get out of here. We'll hike through the woods and camp somewhere. I can't go home now and face my dad and the cops. And that maniac, like you said, might be trying to track us down. Let's hit the road."

Before heading back to town, Officer Matthews stopped by the cabin that had been broken into and returned the stolen items to the owner.

"I located your stolen property, minus the beer," said the officer. "Three boys down the road at a little hunting camp. Boy Scouts, of all people. But teenagers all the same."

"Thank you, officer, for such quick detective work. That sure didn't take you long to figure out."

The man stretched out his hand and shook with the officer, who noted how soiled the man's hands were. "Doing a little gardening?" the officer asked.

"Oh, not really; just a little yard maintenance. The snow will be here before we know it."

The man nodded to the officer and retreated back inside his cabin. After the state police car disappeared, the man waited for a reasonable period to make sure the area was safe. He loaded his .22-caliber rifle and placed it behind his seat in the truck. He wanted to question the boys to see how much they knew, and more importantly, what they had seen.

Back at the camp, the boys swiftly organized their packs, gathered whatever food they could, and hustled down the trail. They came out to a gravel road and followed it for several miles to get far away from the cabin as fast as possible.

After hiking for several hours, they stumbled off to the side of the road, eased their packs to the ground, and sat down in the shade of a maple tree. Chaz unpacked his canteen and took a long, cool drink of water. Jake and Wally spread out a county map on the dry ground and tried to figure out the best escape plan. The boys had very little cash between them and knew they would run out of food within a few days. To survive, they realized they would have to break in again somewhere, someone's camp or house, to steal food supplies. That might be the only way.

As the boys lay there resting, Chaz looked up at the trees silhouetted against the sky and said, "Maybe we should've told the cop about that body and just taken our lumps."

"Yeah, you're probably right," said Jake.

"Oh, great!" said Wally. "I've been telling you guys that all along."

Just as their plan started looking more and more hopeless, a pickup came barreling around the bend toward them. It was too late to load up their packs, so they quickly ran deeper into the woods and lay flat among the trees. The truck pulled up abruptly in a rolling dust cloud, and a man with a rifle jumped out. The man walked over to where the boys had dropped their packs and peered off into the woods.

"All right, boys. C'mon out. I just want to talk to you…. You can't go too far without your packsacks, now can you? All your food and water? No, I don't think so."

The boys lay quietly, not making a sound. They weren't quite sure if this man was the killer, but if he was, and they ran, he could shoot them all one by one.

"You boys must be the ones who broke into my cabin last night. Tell you what; come out here and talk with me, let me ask you a few questions, and I won't press any charges against you. You'll be free to go. I promise . . . scout's honor."

The boys lay motionless in the low bushes, wondering whether to make a run for it into the deeper woods. The man grew agitated waiting for a response. He did not want to be seen by anyone driving by and looked down the road nervously. Turning back toward the boys, he spoke up again.

"All right, boys. That's the game you wanna play, huh? I don't know what you saw, but I know you saw something, and it's not what you think. But let any one of you breathe a word about this to anybody, and I swear I will hunt you down like a jackrabbit and skin you alive. I'll find out who you are and where you live. And I will track you down if it's the last thing I ever do. Remember that!"

As the man turned to walk back to his truck, a skunk appeared not ten feet away and raised its tail toward him. He started to back away quickly but tripped over a tree stump and fell to the ground. The rifle flew into the brush behind him, and in all the excitement, the skunk let loose a powerful torrent of spray, hitting the man directly. As the man rose to his feet, stumbling toward his truck, Jake raced out of the woods and snatched the rifle from the brush. He caught up with the man and pointed the gun at him.

"Throw your truck keys on the ground, or I'll blow your nuts off!" Jake ordered, shaking.

"You wouldn't shoot me, you little weasel," the man said, stinking to high heaven from the new cologne.

"Don't t-test me," Jake stammered, "if you know what's good—good for you."

"You're too chicken-shit," the man said, stumbling awkwardly toward Jake.

Just then, a state police car raced around the bend of the gravel road with its emergency lights flashing. The car ground to a halt, and Officer Matthews approached with his pistol drawn. Pointing it at the man with his hands in the air, he said, "You are under arrest for the murder of your wife." He quickly read him the Miranda rights, slapped a pair of handcuffs on him, and stuffed him into the back of his patrol car.

"Thanks for your help, boys. This one almost got away on me."

Within minutes, Jake's parents' car pulled up on the dusty gravel shoulder. They loaded the boys and their backpacks into the car and headed back toward town. The boys knew there would be a price to pay for the break-in and plenty of explaining to do, but all in all, it was still better than starving and wandering endlessly in the woods.

On the previous Saturday night, a missing person report had been filed by Mrs. McGill's grown daughter. The two were supposed to meet for dinner that evening, but the mother had not shown up. On Sunday, when Officer Matthews got back to his state police post in town, after checking out the break-in at the Raco cabin, he realized Mr. McGill, whom he had recently questioned at the cabin, was the missing woman's husband. He thought back to how soiled the man's hands had seemed. On a strong hunch, Officer Matthews immediately drove back to the Raco cabin and scouted around in the woods nearby. Not sixty yards away from the cabin, he had discovered the body of Mrs. McGill in a shallow grave covered over with leaves and broken sticks. Her wedding ring had been yanked from her finger. When the officer finally caught up with the suspect, he found the ring in Mr. McGill's pocket.

As Mr. McGill later confessed, he and his wife had driven out to the Raco cabin early Saturday afternoon to relax for a few hours. He began drinking whiskey on the rocks as soon as they arrived, one after another. His wife repeatedly berated him for drinking so heavily and poured his bottle down the kitchen sink. In a fit of anger, she also accused him of recently cheating on her with another woman at one of the local bars. She'd heard rumors from her friends for weeks.

Hearing this, Mr. McGill flew into a rage and slapped his wife across the room. She slipped and fell backwards, striking her head on the corner of the metal stove, killing her instantly. Mr. McGill, stunned by her accidental death, thought he would be charged with murder and thrown in jail for years. He had a string of charges on his record, ranging from assault and battery to domestic abuse, and knew the courts would not go easy on him. So, he decided to get rid of the body as quickly as possible, not knowing what he would tell his estranged daughter. The accident had happened late in the day on Saturday, just before dark. Mr. McGill decided he would drive back to town, retrieve a sturdy spade, and bury the body first thing Sunday morning. Meanwhile, he hid the body in the cabin's backroom under a bed.

However, he had not expected intruders while he was gone

and decided he would have to locate any potential witnesses before the cops did. He thought he could intimidate them like he'd intimidated others all his life. It was a wild risk calling the police to investigate a break-in, but that was the only way to find the culprits. If he played his cards carefully, it could all work out smoothly for him. But in the end, it all backfired.

~ ~ ~

In the following weeks, the three boys were punished by their scoutmaster—no promotions or merit badges for the next six months. They were not charged with breaking and entering because of their help solving the murder, but they were nevertheless grounded by their parents for several months.

Later that year, Jake and Chaz regretfully quit the Scouts and, lured by the charms of the feminine persuasion, moved on to greener pastures. They would miss the camping and camaraderie of the troop but welcomed the perks of their growing maturity.

Backbeat

A drummer's job is to drive the beat. Along with the bass player, the drummer in a band powers the pace of the music, keeps the rhythm steady, and ignites people to jump to their feet and crowd the dance floor. Sometimes, all it takes is a pounding 4/4 steady beat on the bass drum to start a song intro and, instantly, the dancers feel the pulse and fly out of their chairs. It's a curious power musicians have over a nightclub crowd, a driving force that can energize the floor. As a band, we've damn near mastered the art.

The four of us have been together for several years, playing weekend gigs at bars and clubs throughout Michigan, mostly in the Upper Peninsula (U.P.). Robbie, our keyboard player, is the latest addition to our band, "Strange Brew." We took that name off an old Eric Clapton album because we liked the way it described our particular style of music, which is eclectic—everything from blues and country to top 40 rock oldies. We play what people like to dance to—mostly Allman Brothers, Springsteen, and Fogelberg. Disco has faded away recently, thank God; we just couldn't bring ourselves to play that stuff. So we play mostly covers and don't have much time to write our own music, but Garret and Henry, our lead guitarist and bass player, collaborate on a few songs of their own.

I go by Willie; my job is to hold the beat together so nobody gets lost. I grew up worshipping drummers like Buddy Rich, Joe Morello, and Gene Krupa. They were such amazing

51

drummers—their speed, control, and overall creativity—great artists to listen to and watch during their solo breaks. Those idols eventually morphed into Ringo, Ginger Baker, and Don Henley. I couldn't seem to get enough of their music.

Like many of the musicians I know, I've dreamed of fame and playing in a big-name band someday or moving out to southern California and becoming a studio-session drummer who records with lots of well-known musicians. People have always told me that to get anywhere in my career, I'd have to leave the U.P. and move to the big city. More job opportunities and connection possibilities. And maybe they're right. But the U.P. is home to me, and I love a lot of things about it—the slower pace, the natural beauty, the lack of crowds. If I had a choice, winter would be a few months shorter and summer a bit longer. I'll have to wait to see how these fuzzy ideas play out.

During the week, we all hold down regular jobs. I work at Sears three days a week, including Saturday, selling and delivering appliances. My boss sends me out Monday afternoons to set up stoves, refrigerators, washers, and dryers. Recently, he said I needed to pick up my sales or he'd have to cut my hours back; he says we're going through a bit of a slump ever since Carter came into office. Since I don't really follow politics much, I have no idea what appliance sales have to do with Washington. It's not my main concern.

Luckily, none of us are married yet, and girlfriends are not exactly hard to find when you're a musician; they're naturally drawn to us. I'm not bragging, just stating the facts. And if we hope to go anywhere as a band, we have to have our freedom—freedom to travel wherever the road takes us.

Maybe we've been playing these small towns for too long. All of us are getting itchy for a change of pace. The other day, at practice, Robbie brought it up again.

"We have to get out of Dodge, guys; I feel the walls closing in. Let's just throw all our instruments and amps in a trailer and head out to Vegas. We could start fresh out there playing the casinos."

"Too many cover bands just like us out there," said Garret. "We'd be just another number in Vegas."

"But if we get a good-paying gig out there," Robbie said, "we'd have more time to write our own music. Don't you guys ever want to break out as a band someday? How will we ever do that playing small-town bars every weekend?"

Garret lit up a smoke, picked up his acoustic Martin, and strummed a few chords. "It's all a crapshoot. A huge roll of the dice. I'm not so sure I'm up for the gamble. Too much to lose." And he expelled a stream of blue smoke from his nostrils.

"We could all find day jobs out there," continued Robbie. "I'd find a gig at a music store teaching keyboards."

The more we talked about moving to Vegas, the more distant it all seemed, like we were simply spinning our wheels. Vegas was a desert mirage that appeared whenever the walls of our small town started closing in. Then, without warning, the idea suddenly vanished. We got caught up in our day-to-day lives with work and women and forgot about it for a while.

My girlfriend, Kayla, waitresses down at The Antlers Restaurant. It's one of the better steakhouses here in the Soo, and she makes good tips. Her dream is to become a professional photographer with her own studio. Kayla wants to go to art school and get her degree. She doesn't mind me playing drums in a band, but I think she knows I'll never make enough to support us if we get married. That's OK; I'm not quite ready to tie the knot anyway.

Sometimes, Kayla gets frustrated with me, and one day, she says, "Willie, do you expect to play drums in a band for the rest of your life? Don't you ever want to do anything else?"

I didn't know what to say. Drums and music are my life; everything revolves around them—until Kayla confronted me. "Sure," I said. "I'm thinking about a few things." At that point, I really didn't have a clue. But things will work out for me; they usually do.

I'd like to go off to college myself someday, maybe study psychology and sociology to help people solve their problems. I'm sure there will never be a shortage of those.

For now, though, the band has a full slate of jobs lined up. Last week, we played Coluzzi's Bar in Manistique. It was the usual Friday/Saturday night gig, and we packed 'em in wall to wall. The dance floor was pumped full of drunken, buzzed-up energy 'til almost 2 a.m. After we finished the last tune on Saturday night, we had a quick beer to cool down, then packed up all the gear and loaded the trailer, ready to depart for home. When the owner of Coluzzi's went to pay us off for the weekend, he pulled a wad of cash from the register and slapped it on the bar.

"Well, boys," he said, "I have to take out $75 for the bar tab you ran up."

"What?" I said. "You told us the drinks were on the house."

I had been ordering Jack Daniels on the rocks as well as longneck beers all weekend, oblivious to the cost, all on the house.

"I said your *first* drink was on the house, not free drinks all night. I'm trying to run a business, not a charity. So here's the balance of what I owe you minus the tab. Take it or leave it."

After chipping in for gas and food all weekend, and drinks,

there wasn't much money left to show for our work. I doubt if we averaged minimum wage. And yet, we had a blast playing music, doing what we loved.

One night, the following winter, we drove three hours west to Negaunee, near Marquette, to play a two-nighter at the L&M Lounge. We hauled the equipment in about 8 p.m. and started setting up to play at 9. A winter storm had swept through the area so bar traffic was sparse. Or, to be more accurate, nonexistent. By 11 p.m., two hours into the gig, there was not a single soul in the place except for the barmaid and a waitress. When we spoke to the manager during a break, he said he'd gotten his dates mixed up and neglected to advertise on the radio that there would be a live band in town. Our show turned out to be a well-kept secret.

The mirrored disco ball spun brilliantly in the middle of an empty dance floor while "Strange Brew" tried its best to entertain the barmaid and waitress. It was a very long night. We tried to think of it as simply a practice. Seeing that faraway look in their eyes, I thought it likely the guys were thinking of putting these small-town gigs behind them and heading out to Vegas.

Above all things, as a band, we have always prided ourselves on being professional. We practice long hours to get down song lyrics, the right chords, guitar leads, and vocal harmonies. And we put energy and passion into every song we play. But, sometimes, we mess things up.

Most gigs we play require some long, tedious hours of driving. To pass the time, we all toke up a little to get in the right frame of mind. Not too much, just enough to get a buzz on. This one particular night, everything was getting pretty hot on the dance floor, the rowdy crowd really digging the music. During one song, Henry must have toked a few too many puffs. He got lost in the wrong key, forgot the lyrics to the song, and screwed up his solo. First time I'd ever seen him mess up so badly. He just smiled wanly at the rest of us as if to say, "Whatever."

After the night ended, as we were packing up our equipment, Garret read Henry the riot act. "Listen; don't you ever fuck up like that again or you'll be out of this band for good! If you get so high that you can't play right, you'll be history in a heartbeat!"

Henry walked away without a word. It was a long night's drive back to the Soo, in almost total silence. He never messed up like that again.

When the following summer finally came around, Robbie and Garret had worked up some new material to record. A studio over in Marquette had agreed to work with us for a split of the proceeds. The first track we recorded for a two-sided 45 record was "Endless Romance," a tender ballad about love and heartache. The other track was an upbeat rock-n-roll number called "Don't Stop Dancing." It's heavy on percussion and screaming guitar solos and really rocks.

We immediately hit all the radio stations across the U.P. and Northern Michigan and talked up the tracks with local deejays. Luckily, we scored a number of radio interviews and small-newspaper stories. For a while, we felt like celebrities with our friends and fans, even charging a little more to play out. Record promotion can be an exciting business, and the band was finally getting some traction and a name. But it can quickly wear you out and strip all the pleasure out of playing music itself. There's only so much time in a day, and we were exhausted from the hectic pace of promotion.

At last, good news! We got a call from an agent who'd listened to our new record on the radio. He was interested in representing us. According to him, he was tied in with the Holiday Inn hotel chain and could line up four to six months' work playing lounges all over the Midwest. He insisted we wear matching outfits on stage to look more polished and professional: something like purple shirts with black vests and white slacks. Maybe this would be a major stepping stone to the next level. It would certainly be quite a change-up from our current wardrobe of T-shirts and blue jeans.

During the next couple of months, we played every Friday and Saturday night, getting home about 3 or 4 a.m. That was starting to get old for a few of us who had to be to work by 8 a.m. The idea of going on the road for months at a time appealed to everyone but me. Moneywise, it would probably be a break-even deal at best. Expenses would eat up all the profits. But it was a possible way of getting our name out there. Kayla wasn't too hot on the idea of my being away for many months, and I didn't really want to leave her alone. We'd been together too long.

Finally, we decided as a band to go for broke. Strange Brew hit the road for the next six months, playing the night club circuit, including Holiday Inn lounges, five nights a week. Maybe, we thought, we would catch a lucky break and be *discovered* by a big-name record label and signed to a recording contract. It was worth a gamble. We had all quit our day jobs at home and committed as a band to promoting ourselves on the road.

We played small towns and larger cities from Detroit and Chicago to St. Louis and Minneapolis. After three or four months, it was starting to get old. The glamour was quickly fading. In several cities, we had been approached by local DJs who offered to play our new 45, but we didn't get any callbacks or new recording opportunities. We felt like we were simply grinding it out, day after day. Then, to make matters worse, one night after a weekend gig near Milwaukee, we were loading our trailer, and while we walked back into the lounge for a final check, someone stole two Les Paul guitars and a Fender amp. All within a minute's time. It was a major downer, setting us back several thousand dollars, so we had to get an advance from our agent to replace our instruments.

To save money, we stayed in cramped motel rooms and ate mostly at fast-food joints. After nearly six months of playing night after night on the road, we were starting to get on each other's nerves.

"This road gig," said Henry, "is really starting to suck. We're not making any serious money or getting anywhere new as a band."

Garret flopped down on the hotel bed. "Money?" he said. "Whoever said anything about making big money? All we wanted was a little fame in the music business, just a small slice of the pie. Turns out musicians like us are a dime a dozen. We're expendable."

Not long after that, we quit the road gig and headed back to the Soo. The band split up, and we all went separate ways. I joined a country band for a few months, then a blues band, but nothing seemed to gel. The road had beaten the dream out of us.

Henry, our bass player, had been the first one to leave our band for another local group. He claimed to have artistic differences, but the last straw for him was that we had to wear matching outfits when we played on the road. That was a line he could no longer cross—too regimented and suffocating, he felt. "I'll never wear ruffled shirts and matching bowties again. We're not The Temptations, for God's sake." It would kill his mojo, he claimed, so he split.

Last I heard about Henry, his girlfriend was pregnant, and

he had quit his band to find a better-paying job. He wanted to get married and find a bigger place to live before the baby arrived. Rumor was he wanted to move to Nashville to try his luck. Henry had switched completely from rock and blues to pure country. I didn't see that coming, but I hope he makes it.

When the band broke up, Robbie and Garret decided it was time to make their break. They headed out to LA to check out the music scene, and if that didn't work out, Vegas was not that far away. These two had a truckload of talent and made a great songwriting team, even if they weren't quite of Lennon-McCartney caliber. If things fell apart, they could always return to the Soo to regroup. In a way, I really envied them. They had more balls than most small-town musicians.

Kayla and I decided to get married and moved up to Marquette to attend college. She had come a long way with her photography, having won several regional photo competitions, and wanted to pursue it further. So she applied for admission to Northern's art department.

I finally gave up the glitz and glamour of trying to become some kind of rock star. The whole idea now seemed unrealistic and overrated. I haven't completely abandoned music, though; I've simply readjusted my goals to something more down-to-earth. So I'm currently pursuing a university degree in music and thinking about teaching someday.

I wasn't ready to give up drumming, but I was putting it on hold for a while. I love music and jamming with other musicians, but I had to make room for other things in my life. For now, being married to Kayla is keeping me grounded and focused. If we ever have kids, I hope they're interested in music so I can teach them everything I know.

We had a great band together for a few years, a very tight relationship, and worked hard at it. I gradually came to realize great musicians are plentiful everywhere you go, and only a handful of them ever make a big name for themselves. Success seems so fickle, so random, at times. Yet you still need considerable talent while you're waiting for lightning to strike. As for me, I'm still driving the beat—but this time, dancing to a different drummer.

Street Smart

It wasn't so much the uniform that impressed Rachel as the opportunity to make a difference in someone's life. Ever since she was a child, she had always wanted to study law enforcement and join the police force. To Rachel, the world was not divided between good guys and bad guys, right and wrong, so much as it was a sea of gray, a mix of unfortunate circumstances and missed opportunities.

Rachel had grown up watching old *Perry Mason* episodes on TV as well as her favorites, *Hill Street Blues* and *CSI*. If you fitted most of the pieces together—and were persistent— the puzzle usually solved itself. And yet, as she soon learned, things were not always what they seemed. If you looked beneath the surface, many criminals were very complicated people who grew up in abusive households, hung around with dangerous individuals, or had alcoholic fathers who were absent most of the time. Rachel had always felt that, given a better influence or opportunity here or there, most criminals would never have become involved with the legal system. If she was ever hired onto the police force, she vowed to change people's lives, one person at a time.

At age thirty-five, Rachel had returned to school at Michigan State to study law enforcement. She had started out years earlier as a sociology major, intent on helping individuals who had fallen through the cracks, but she had drifted away, unsure of her direction. Rachel had never felt a need to get married and did not feel any strong maternal urge to have children. Her friends often wondered about her choice but accepted that she was perfectly happy with her life. Rachel sought fulfillment in other ways.

To afford her part-time classes, Rachel waitressed at the All Day Café some mornings and a few weekend evenings during the dinner rush. Tony, her boss, who had been running the café for more than ten years, had expanded his menu from morning toast-and-eggs to lunchtime sandwiches-and-pie and finally to dinnertime roast beef-and-mashed-potatoes with gravy. It wasn't fancy, but the locals loved it and provided a steady and dependable clientele.

The customers liked Rachel's friendly chit-chat and clever comebacks, and tipped her accordingly. Every night when she came home, Rachel tossed an apron-full of tips into a large Maxwell House can on top of the refrigerator. Most of it would go toward books and tuition and occasionally a night out on the town with friends.

One afternoon on her way home, after working the break-fast and lunch rush, Rachel walked past a homeless man on the sidewalk. He wore a threadbare army fatigue jacket and a Tigers baseball cap and squatted on a slab of cardboard next to his shopping cart full of empty bottles. She'd seen the man several times before but neglected to stop—fearful of talking to strangers, especially homeless ones. Today, when she saw this lonely figure, she felt sorry for him and decided to stop and say hello.

"Ma'am, can you spare a quarter for a guy down on his luck?" he asked.

Rachel reached for some of her tip money in her apron and dropped it into his empty cup. "Are you hungry?" she asked.

"When was the last time you ate?"

"Haven't had much today, miss, not even a cup of coffee."

Rachel handed him the bag containing her cheeseburger and apple pie she had planned to take home for dinner. The man ripped the bag open and quickly devoured the offering.

"What's your name anyway?" she asked. "I see you out here just about every day."

"Name's Lenny. I used to be a pretty good carpenter 'til I fell off a scaffold on the job. Can't work like I used to." He seemed to perk up a little after the burger and pie.

"Well, Lenny, have you been out on the street for quite a while?"

"Going on six months now. After I was injured and couldn't work, my wife ran off with another fellow, but before she disappeared, she emptied our bank account. No need to feel sorry for me; I'm managing all right."

So many people were afraid of talking to homeless people on the street. If they weren't high on drugs, they were buzzed on cheap alcohol, but Lenny seemed different.

"Where were you living at the time?" Rachel asked, and suddenly, she felt she was getting too nosey. "I'm sorry. It's really none of my business."

"No, miss. It's quite all right. I don't get to talk to people anymore. They mostly ignore me and cross the street. I don't like being out here on the street much, but after being out of work, I couldn't afford the bills, and the bank took over my house."

"I'm sorry for that, Lenny, but I really should be going. It's been good talking to you. See you around." She wanted to know more about Lenny, but she felt she was being intrusive.

Lenny watched Rachel walk down the sidewalk and around the corner. In a small way, she had brightened his day, and he smiled to himself. As a homeless person, he was used to being ignored.

In the weeks that followed, Rachel tried to stop by Lenny's regular location whenever she could and drop off some sandwiches and coffee. By late October, the days were cooling off, and she wondered what Lenny would do when winter arrived. Between her classes and working at the café, she had very little time for herself.

One afternoon at the café, after the lunch crowd had thinned out, Rachel was ringing up one of her last customers at the register. The door jerked open and in stumbled a man wearing a black watch cap and with a handkerchief over his face. He lunged toward the register and pointed what looked like a replica of a pistol at Rachel.

"Don't move!" he ordered. "Just empty the register very carefully into this bag!" His voice was muffled behind the handkerchief.

Rachel froze for a moment, but she did as he asked. She looked at the man's eyes and seemed to note something familiar. The gunman would not return her stare but looked away nervously.

"Hurry it up!" he barked.

As Rachel stuffed all the coins and bills into his bag, she glanced up at him again and noticed a small anchor tattoo on the side of his neck. Months earlier, Lenny had mentioned to her that his anchor tattoo was from one drunken night uptown in Cleveland when he was sailing as a watchman on the freighters. The gunman grabbed the bag of cash, bolted out the café door, and fled down the sidewalk into a back alley.

When the police arrived a few minutes later, Rachel filled them in on most of the details of the robbery, but she did not mention the tattoo. She was too stunned, knowing Lenny had robbed her boss of close to $200, and at gunpoint, even though she was fairly certain the gun was fake. What was he thinking? She was angry and disappointed in him. Part of her wanted to have him picked up and thrown in jail. But if she did that, he'd be behind bars for at least the next ten years. Was there some other way?

Rachel walked home a different way for the next couple of weeks, avoiding the place where Lenny hung out. She couldn't face him without saying something. Not now anyway.

She had a hard time sleeping at night, thinking about the robbery. Focusing on her classes and studying was nearly impossible. What police force would ever hire her if they discovered she had withheld information on a robbery suspect? She was jeopardizing her future, and all for what? Maybe Lenny had left town after the robbery and was halfway across the country. But no, she thought, he had seemed like a decent man when she met him; something must have snapped.

The next morning, Rachel skipped class and headed down the block to see if Lenny was still around. This time she brought no coffee or sandwiches. He was in his usual spot, shaking a few coins in his tin cup as she approached.

"Well, good morning, Miss Rachel. You don't look all that happy today. Something bothering you?"

Her arms folded, Rachel stared back at him coldly. "I think you know exactly what's bothering me," she said.

The easy-going smile disappeared from Lenny's face. "What do you mean?"

"The robbery at the café—I know it was you. I recognized

your voice, and that anchor tattoo on your neck gave you away. But I haven't told anyone yet. So why did you do it? What were you thinking?"

Lenny hung his head and stared down at the leaves swirling on the sidewalk. He could feel her disappointment. "I'm sorry. I shouldn't have done it, but I was feeling desperate. Too many nights sleeping under newspapers and cardboard on the streets. I guess I just wanted a couple nights in a warm motel and some good food. Why didn't you turn me in?"

"I'm taking a gamble on you. I thought maybe what you needed was a break, a second chance. You seemed to me like a good man with a good heart . . . . Tell you what, Lenny. I'll make you a deal."

He looked at her suspiciously. "What kind of deal?"

Rachel stepped close to him and calmly looked him in the eye. "You stole $200 from my boss, and I expect you to pay it back. If I turn you in, you're going to the slammer for a good ten years, even though that was not a real gun you used. Still interested?"

Recognizing his limited options, he nodded. "OK, but where am I going to get $200 cash and still have enough to eat on?"

"You're going to have to work it off, little by little. I'll pay you $10 an hour for some painting and odd jobs I need done around the house."

For the next several weeks, Lenny worked at Rachel's house two to three days a week when the weather was good. She had him start off by scraping, priming, and painting her flaking windowsills and trim. Then he reglued the loose rungs on a rocking chair and fixed a wobbly coffee table. One day, he showed up with a jack plane and trimmed down a sticking front door that wouldn't close properly. On his final day of work, Lenny rebuilt the set of wooden steps leading into the front porch and repainted an old chest of drawers in the bedroom.

Lenny showed great pride and enthusiasm in every project he was given. His craftsmanship was superb. Rachel was impressed by both his eclectic skills and his work ethic. His low spirits seemed to have lifted.

"You're really amazing with your tools," she said. "I didn't realize you had such a knack for woodworking."

"Chip off the old block, I guess. My dad was always a wiz around the house fixing things. Glad I saved all my carpentry tools; I stashed 'em with a friend when I lost my house. Thought they might come in handy someday."

The day after Rachel paid Lenny off, he wrote a short note to her employer, apologizing for the robbery, and stuffed $200 in cash into an envelope and dropped it that night through the mail slot at the All Day Café. With a clear conscience, he felt hopeful there were better days to come. He could see possibilities that had not existed in a long while.

Not far from Lenny's familiar panhandling street corner, Rachel was able to locate a shelter for him to sleep at temporarily. She had helped him find a part-time job at a local ready-to-finish furniture store. He was responsible for assembling wood furniture, applying finishes, and repairing occasional pieces that customers brought in. He had been knocked down for quite a while, but thanks to Rachel, he could feel his second wind coming on.

Lenny's back injuries were slowly healing, and he hoped to return soon to his carpentry trade, building and remodeling homes. He considered fine-tuning his skills and becoming a finish carpenter, hanging cabinets and doors and trimming out the woodwork in various rooms. There were more than enough rough carpenters in the world, he figured, but far fewer skilled craftsmen.

2
PURSUIT

Slow Dance

Back in high school, Paul had never learned how to dance with girls. He always attended the mixers after football and basketball games where, in subdued gymnasium lights, live bands mesmerized the crowd with their covers of current top 40 hits. The girls were achingly beautiful, Paul thought, the cheerleaders untouchable. Fast dancing was out of the question—he felt much too awkward. But learning to slow dance was not out of the question; that didn't look too difficult.

The night seemed to pass so quickly, and he couldn't get up the nerve to ask anyone for a slow dance. *What if she turns me down? I'd be mortified forever.* Paul had his eye on a cute blond with long curly hair who was over in the corner talking with her friends. His heart was pounding as he rehearsed his opening line in his head: *Would you like to dance?* He tried not to stare at her, though she was quite pretty. *Stop staring. She'll think you're stalking her.* Even though she was in his third-hour biology class, he had never spoken to her. He popped a Tic Tac in his mouth for good breath and started nonchalantly across the dance floor. Suddenly, the bright lights in the gymnasium came on, the band thanked everyone for coming, and the night was over. Paul was angry with himself for hesitating too long; he grabbed his coat and walked home alone.

~ ~ ~

After graduating from high school, Paul began working

for his dad in the stone business. His father ran an independent shop engraving cemetery headstones, or monuments, as they were called in the trade. It was heavy-duty labor lifting the marble and granite slabs and very dusty sandblasting the names, dates, and intricate designs. Paul's dad trained him to be extremely careful in laying out a stone for engraving to avoid any misspelling of names or mix-ups on dates. One small error and the precious stone was a total waste, hundreds of dollars quickly thrown away.

In the summer and fall, Paul delivered the finished stone markers to various cemeteries around the Eastern Upper Peninsula. His dad's old Ford pickup had a small hydraulic winch to maneuver the heavy marble slabs for loading in and out of the truck. Sometimes, Paul couldn't locate the sexton at a particular cemetery to show him where to place the marker. In that case, he made his best guess, according to his dad's instructions, and went to work. Now and then, Paul positioned the stone marker over the wrong grave and had to return weeks later to relocate it properly. It was back-breaking work, but Paul liked the freedom and independence of his job.

Business was steady all summer until just after Halloween, when the ground became too frozen to deal with, and burials came to a halt. Cemeteries were soon snowed in for the next six months. Nevertheless, the engraving went on all winter long, but at a slower pace.

To compensate for the diminished income, Paul began cutting firewood on state land and selling it locally. After the expense of gas and a chainsaw, there wasn't a great deal of profit left over. But the winter seemed to pass much faster.

By mid-February, the snow had piled up outside, and the temperatures had plummeted to below zero. For a change of pace, Paul decided to check out the Alpha Addition, a popular local nightclub that had a live band on Saturday nights. The drinks were reasonable, and a bevy of attractive ladies always filled the dance floor. Paul met his friend Dave there that night, ordered beers, and surveyed the array of women from the corner of the bar.

In the dimly lit room, red and blue beams bouncing off the mirrored ball overhead, Paul felt uneasy and self-conscious. The music blasting from the bandstand was so loud he could barely hear himself think. Maybe it was his stiff Kmart blue jeans or his J.C. Penney's work boots, but he soon noticed most of the guys dancing with women had a much classier style and taste in their wardrobes. Their dress was sportier and more refined than what he was offering. Even Dave seemed to notice.

"Yeah, Paul, if you want to have any luck with these women, you're going to have to up your game a little. Sharpen it up a bit, and lose the hunting boots."

"What? These are my everyday shoes."

"Well, you can't dance in those. You look like you're ready to bale hay. Trust me; looks matter when it comes to women."

Paul watched Dave wander across the dance floor to talk to a couple girls who were laughing about something. As Dave approached, one of the girls appeared to look him over approvingly and winked back at her friend. Within a few minutes, he was out on the floor, slow dancing with one of them. To Dave, talking to women seemed so effortless, like he had done it all his life.

Paul leaned on the bar, nervously sipping his beer, wanting to start up a conversation with a girl. But he couldn't seem to summon the nerve. He had never dated a girl back in high school, although he had wanted to many times. His shyness had stopped him in his tracks. He was afraid he might say the wrong thing, something totally embarrassing.

When Dave came back to the bar, Paul asked him, "Why is it always so easy for you? Talking to girls, making small talk, you're such a pro. Don't you ever get nervous or tongue-tied?"

"It's not as hard as you think. You just walk up to them and make a comment or joke of some kind. Get a reaction from them. Then smile and introduce yourself."

"Oh, yeah," said Paul. "That sounds real easy. I'd probably forget my own name. What if you just run out of things to say to her?"

Dave laughed. "You never run out. Just ask her a few things about herself. Women love to talk about themselves. All you need to do is listen and nod your head once in a while, like you're hanging on every word."

Paul didn't dance with anyone that night, but thanks to Dave, he felt he had learned something about women. To him, it was like trying to pick a lock blindfolded. He hadn't quite developed the light touch, but he was determined to improve.

After work one day, on a friend's suggestion, Paul went home and logged on to Weekends.com, a popular dating website. Ever since Paul had invested a few dollars in an updated wardrobe and a new haircut, he was feeling more confident. After filling out his profile and uploading his picture, he was able to chat online with a few ladies who seemed like possibilities. When they asked what he did for a living and he answered honestly that he engraved cemetery markers, they seemed to quickly lose interest. They wanted to know what kind of salary he earned, but Paul was vague in his reply, feeling that was too personal. The whole Weekends.com experience seemed creepy to him, people pretending to be someone else. Apparently, every person online was the perfect catch—no warts, no flaws, no misdemeanors. It all seemed so distant and pretentious, and after a few evenings on his computer, Paul gave up. There had to be an easier way to meet girls.

After work, Paul stopped at the grocery store to pick up something for dinner. He had cooked enough chili, tacos, and frozen pizza lately; it was time for some pan-fried whitefish. Walking up to the fresh fish display, he noticed a wide variety of salmon, trout, herring, and whitefish spread out on a bed of crushed ice. A young woman, standing a few feet from Paul, was staring into the fish case.

"Do you know anything about cooking fish?" she asked. "I have no idea, but I want to try something new tonight."

The girl looked to be in her early twenties, slim-built, red-haired, and lightly complected. She glanced at Paul with inquisitive blue eyes and smiled.

"Oh, me?" Paul stammered. "It's really not hard—a little flour, salt, and pepper, and you cook 'em in some hot oil, but not too long."

"What kind of fish would you recommend?"

"The whitefish, definitely. They're locally caught and very tasty with some fresh lemon and tartar sauce." Paul felt confident that he knew what he was talking about. It seemed so different from his awkwardness at the night club.

"Thanks. By the way, my name's Felicia."

"Oh, I'm Paul, and I'm in the market for whitefish, too. I've been catching mostly perch this winter out in the bay, but only a few whitefish."

"You fish in one of those little black ice shacks? How cool."

Paul was beaming, hesitated for a second, then leapt in. "My shack is all heated and sitting in about five feet of water. You can see all the fish swimming beneath you."

"Wow. That sounds so exciting."

"Yeah, it's a blast.... If you'd ever be interested in giving it a try, I could take you out there sometime. Only takes a few minutes to ride out there on my snowmobile."

Within a few minutes, Paul had lined up his first date, a morning of ice-fishing in his shack on the upper St. Mary's River. Either the planets had aligned correctly or Paul's luck was changing. Call it random chance or serendipity, his life was suddenly full of possibility.

On a cold Saturday morning as the sun broke across the river, Paul and Felicia sped across the ice on his Arctic Cat and pulled up to his fish shack. It was late February and the ice was more than twelve inches thick. Paul chipped away the skim ice over the hole and lit the propane stove. The bright sunshine bounced off the sandy bottom beneath the shack where Paul had scattered a can of kernel corn. Most fishermen believed the feed attracted more fish to the neighborhood and served as a good luck charm.

Before long, it was warm enough to remove their winter jackets. Paul showed Felicia how to attach wax worms to the small hooks and gently jig the pole to attract attention. She seemed intrigued by the whole process and curious about every detail. In the crystal clear lake water beneath the shack, a couple of menominee soon swam under the hole, nosed the bait, and drifted away.

"They don't seem too hungry yet," Paul said. "We might have to wait a while."

"That's OK. This is all so beautiful," said Felicia, "like having your own personal aquarium. I'll bet you never get tired of this."

"Never. It's one thing I love about winter on Lake Superior.

Every time a fish swims past the hole, my heart beats faster. Watching them swim under the ice and how they react to the bait is half the fun."

When a couple of whitefish swam over to nibble on the corn, Felicia focused her camera and took a few shots. "This is for a photography class I'm taking up at the college."

"Oh, I didn't know you were in school."

"My senior year. I'm an art major concentrating on painting and sculpture. You work with marble; I work with alabaster. It's a slow-working medium, but I love it."

Paul jigged his line a little and stared down into the icy water. "Stone is such an unforgiving material," said Paul. "You make one mistake and it's ruined. There's no patching it up."

"That's part of the excitement, isn't it? The tension of working with this material—one false move and it's over. But the potential for beauty is endless."

"To me, it's a way to make a living," Paul replied. "And moving granite and marble slabs around all day gets a little tiring sometimes."

"Yes," Felicia said, "but the work you do in stone is like an art form. You aren't just engraving names and dates; you are creating works of art that will last forever. Your skills and craftsmanship make all the difference. It's the last loving thing you can do to honor someone who has died. Look at the works of Michelangelo or Rodin—they're eternal."

Paul hadn't quite thought of his work that way, but he admired Felicia's passion and the way her eyes lit up when she spoke. She asked about his dreams and life aspirations, where he'd like to travel to, and what his ideal day would look like.

She asked him about things he hadn't really considered very deeply and seemed to stir something in him that had not existed before. Her easy-going manner chased away his shyness and self-consciousness. It was like talking to an old friend.

By noon, they had done more talking than fishing, but they managed to hook one whitefish and a couple of menominee. He liked her quirky sense of humor and the way she laughed so easily at some of his lame jokes. She liked his modesty and quiet sense of confidence. He hadn't come across as a guy trying to impress her or brag about his accomplishments. She agreed to meet him for dinner the following weekend.

Just after 8 p.m. on Saturday, Paul and Felicia went to dinner at Angio's, a small Italian restaurant out by the Plaza. They ordered red wine along with rigatoni, salad, and crusty Italian bread. During a lull in the conversation, Felicia reached into a bag beneath the table and pulled out a package.

"A little surprise for you. I've been working on it all week," she said.

Paul slowly unwrapped what looked like an 11 x 14 photograph that had been altered. She had added color and texture to the image of fish swimming beneath his shack. The scene had a golden iridescence to it.

"It's breathtaking," said Paul. "I can't believe you did this from a photo."

Paul remembered the small package he had brought with him. "And something for you," he said. "I've been thinking of you quite a bit."

For such a little package, it was fairly heavy. Felicia pulled out a slender slab of granite that had been polished and engraved in small letters: DREAM. She smiled at him.

"You made me consider," Paul said, "that we have more

possibilities in us than we ever realize."

They both laughed and toasted to their friendship.

Six weeks later, in the spring, Paul was invited to Felicia's senior art exhibit at the college gallery. She was showing her best work from the past few years, from nature photography to portrait paintings and abstract stone sculptures. Paul was quite impressed with her portfolio.

"I had no idea you were this talented. You seem so humble, but you are truly amazing. What do you plan to do with all this artistic ability?"

"Thanks, but I'm not totally sure of my next direction. I'd like to work in some sort of art gallery and set up my own studio. Whether I can make a living off my work is anyone's guess."

"Well, now you've got me rethinking my priorities," said Paul. "Maybe someday we can collaborate on a project."

"I would really like that."

She smiled sweetly and he kissed her on the cheek. *This relationship,* Paul thought, *is so much like a slow dance. You have to feel the music and take one thing at a time–no point in rushing. It's not quite as scary as it once seemed. Just follow the rhythm and try not to step on her toes.*

The Numbers Game

Ever since he was a kid, Nathan Kelly had been good with numbers. He was born with the ability to add, subtract, and multiply numbers in his head faster than anyone could squeeze the answer from a calculator. He memorized baseball and football statistics and could accurately predict the odds of which team would win. Once he got to college, he became even more intrigued by the world of numbers. There was an intoxicating mystery about them that fascinated him.

Winters in Marquette, Michigan, were snow-packed and never-ending, which gave Nathan all the more reason to focus on his studies at Northern Michigan University. He had enrolled in NMU's accounting program in the early 2000s and taken classes in statistics, probability, and business. In his odd hours, he studied *The Wall Street Journal* and the stock market. Sometimes, he dreamed of becoming a stock market millionaire through shrewd investments and writing bestsellers about his phenomenal market discoveries. That would all come in time, he figured, but for now, all he wanted was to become a CPA with an accounting degree. In no time at all, Wall Street would be knocking down his door for savvy financial advice and begging him to join their firm.

After graduating, Nathan married Maya, a very extroverted and spontaneous girl he had met in a psychology class. She was a music major who wanted to teach elementary students. She loved young children and hoped to find a job locally.

Despite the endless winters, Nathan and Maya both loved the summers and falls in Marquette. It was a beautiful area for hiking and canoeing, and to them, long winters were simply the price they paid to enjoy good weather the rest of the year.

They located a first-floor apartment on Third Street, just a few blocks' walk to downtown on Washington and Front. Walking would save them gas money and provide a little exercise. They were budgeting their funds until they could get solidly on their feet.

By September, Maya had found a teaching job in the local schools, and Nathan had landed part-time work at the accounting firm of T&M Tax Prep doing business taxes for clients and training new employees on how to do personal returns for customers. Springtime was the big rush for taxes, and his job was to prepare for that event.

Within three years, they had saved enough to put a down payment on a small bungalow on Ohio Street. Nathan and Maya were not ready to have children for several more years, preferring to establish their career roots first. By saving a little each week, they were able to afford a ten-year-old Toyota so Maya could drive to work. Nathan would much rather walk the ten blocks to his office downtown. It gave him a chance to clear his head and prepare for the day.

Despite two jobs between them, money always seemed tight. What with car insurance, repairs, utility bills, food, and paying off student loans, there wasn't much left at the end of the month. Nathan hadn't received much of a raise in the past couple of years, so he decided to look for a better-paying job. Unless they bought a second car, the job would have to be within walking distance.

After work one afternoon, Nathan borrowed the car from Maya and drove over to Super One to pick up some things for dinner. He had a short list of items in his pocket and was very selective with his purchases. As he placed a bag of brown rice in his cart, he made a mental note: $1.19. Romaine lettuce: $.99. Pork chops: $4.56. Toilet paper: $1.99. By the time he got to the checkout, Nathan had over a dozen items in his cart. Before the cashier could ring up any of his items on the register, Nathan quickly wrote out his check for the exact amount. When the cashier finally tallied up the bill, she said, "That'll be $24.73, sir." He held the check out to her for exactly $24.73. "Well," she said, "that was a lucky guess."

"No luck, ma'am," he said, smiling, "just numbers."

Within a short time, Nathan received a call from one of Marquette's most reputable hotels, Superior Lodge. It had more than fifty rooms, several suites, a seafood restaurant, and an entertainment lounge that featured a piano player on weekends. Nathan was hired to manage the hotel's bookkeeping and payroll. The hotel was located on 41 as you drive into town, a thirty-minute walk from home, and he had been offered slightly higher pay than the previous job.

In less than six months, Nathan had familiarized himself with the hotel's procedures and systems and seemed to get along well with the management. They found that he had streamlined and simplified some of the business' more unwieldy details and accounting methods and smoothed out many of the bumps and snags. He was soon given more responsibilities as well as a modest salary increase.

But Nathan wasn't completely happy. He liked his job and worked very hard at it, but something seemed to be missing in his life. There weren't enough highlights and bold experiences, just the daily grind of working. His relationship had grown stale and needed rejuvenation. Maya was quite busy, too, with her teaching job, always preparing materials for class every evening. *Maybe,* he thought, *we need a vacation somewhere to spend more time together.* It would have to be in the summer when Maya was free from school. Perhaps a sailing trip off Cape Cod or a white-water rafting trip down the Colorado River.

Nathan liked security and predictability in his life the same way he liked predictability in numbers. Math held an elegant beauty, just like nature. He believed a specific reason always existed for why things worked out a certain way–not by chance and certainly not by accident. No gray areas to worry about–numbers were exact. At the same time, Nathan craved an element of excitement, a bit of risk-taking to add another dimension to his very predictable, buttoned-down existence.

Nathan knew if he and Maya had more money, they'd be investing in stocks, playing the options market, or buying commodities like pork bellies or corn futures. They'd be moving up the financial ladder in no time. But there was no excess money; every dollar seemed to be spoken for. They would probably have to borrow money at the bank to go on a summer vacation. With the high interest rate on their Visa card, they didn't dare put any loans on their plastic. Banks certainly knew how to manipulate numbers, Nathan thought, and a credit card loan would be a losing proposition.

Unexpected expenses came out of the blue. The Toyota needed repairs on the brakes and transmission, which had been put off long enough. Then Maya developed some serious dental problems and needed two crowns and a filling. Their plans for a summer vacation began to drift away like a kite in the wind.

The more Nathan played with numbers, the more he thought he could manipulate them to his advantage. For him, it became a game of staying one step ahead of the system. At work, the management at Superior Lodge seemed to trust him to a great extent. He had worked the bugs out of their financial procedures and put them on a sound footing. But there were little glitches in the system, holes that only Nathan was aware of.

At first, he moved the numbers around very gradually. He didn't think of it as stealing because he planned to pay it all back eventually. To him, it was merely an interest-free loan to be paid back at his convenience. It wasn't really his fault, Nathan thought, that he had mounting car-repair bills, dental expenses, and other unexpected obligations.

At home, Maya was growing restless during a particularly warm summer stretch. "Why don't we go somewhere, Nathan? Let's get out of town for a few days and go down to Traverse City or visit some friends in the Soo?"

Nathan knew she was right. Except for an odd weekend here or there, they hadn't really traveled anywhere in more than three years; they couldn't really afford to. But he was determined to find a way.

As Nathan pored over the receipts and payables from various sections of the hotel operations, he thought of a subtle way to alter the numbers. He had daily receipts from room rentals, the restaurant, the gift shop, and the lounge. By slightly underreporting the money from any one of these areas, he was able to skim off the difference and deposit it digitally in his own bank account. He would then make the normal daily entries on the books, and nothing seemed out of place.

At first, Nathan changed numbers only once a week, but soon it was every other day. Soon, he came up with a way to skim from customers' credit cards when they were booking rooms, by slightly overcharging them and pocketing the difference. The technique was nearly seamless–$5 or $10 at a time, but it returned a tidy profit for his efforts.

After several months of saving in a separate bank account, Nathan ordered a new dining set, a sofa and loveseat, and a big-screen TV for the house. When the pieces were delivered, Maya was happy about the new furniture but disappointed that she hadn't been allowed to have any input on their styles or colors. Nathan hugged her and said, "I just wanted to surprise you all at once." She smiled at the new additions to the house and forgave him.

After Christmas, the snow in Marquette began piling up very quickly. Nathan shoveled his driveway every other day, trying to keep up with it. By late February, he began to think winter might never end. He grew restless and had difficulty sleeping most nights. At times, he would creep downstairs at 3 a.m. and read his financial magazines to tire himself out.

Some nights when he couldn't sleep, he made an excuse to Maya about going to visit some friends and drove up to the casino. He studied the blackjack tables and his favorite slot machines, trying to figure out what would give him the best odds. The first few nights that he gambled, he walked away several hundred dollars poorer. Then, on another night, he lucked out at blackjack and came away with a couple of thousand. It was sheer euphoria to Nathan, an impressive psychic reward for simply playing a shrewd numbers game. For a moment, he considered taking his winnings and quietly paying back the hotel in full for the money he had skimmed. He'd be free and clear of all obligations. Instead, he decided to treat his wife and himself to a well-deserved vacation. He would plan a river-rafting trip through the Grand Canyon during mid-August. The anticipation and planning would get them both through the remainder of the long, brutal winter.

By the time spring arrived in the U.P., Nathan's luck had changed. At the casino, where he hung out several nights a week, he began to lose much more than he had won. He played the $10 and $25 slots more often, but seemed to have hit a cold streak. He had calculated the odds on each machine, but the odds had deserted him. They were usually predictable over a certain period of time, but now and then, betting on the odds would take a long, unexpected turn, and it rattled Nathan. To calm himself, he began drinking whiskey shots and beer chasers. Some nights, he didn't get home until 3 a.m. and had to be to work by 8.

After his recent gambling losses and the many late nights out at the casino, Nathan seemed to be growing distant in his relationship. Most nights he had stopped kissing his wife goodnight and simply staggered into bed without a word. Maya began to suspect something unusual about Nathan's recent behavior and asked about it. He tried to placate her concerns with gifts of jewelry and frequent nights out at the best restaurants in town. She enjoyed the pampered treatment but started to wonder where all the money was suddenly coming from. Nathan simply told her he had won big at the casino, though he was actually going deeper and deeper in the hole. Gradually, he was skimming more money from the hotel to cover his gambling losses. To himself, he made a pledge that with the next big casino win he would pay back the money he had borrowed. He had not meant for things to go this far, but he had every intention of making matters right.

One weekend, Nathan went car shopping by himself. He traded in their old Toyota for a vintage Ford Mustang in mint condition. It was cherry red with leather bucket seats and a stick shift. Maya loved it but wondered how they could afford it. Their friends gathered around and admired the new hotrod in the driveway. Nathan grinned and said it was all thanks to his recent promotion at Superior Lodge. His buddies envied how swiftly he was moving up in the world.

Unfortunately, things were not going so well back at the

hotel. Creditors and vendors who had not been paid began calling Nathan about delinquent invoices. He sent checks to the noisiest ones but found ways to prolong payments to the others. Complaining of lost invoices, Nathan asked to be sent new copies. To others, he promised to put a check in the mail within the week.

This arrangement went on for quite some time, but before long, creditors wanted to speak with Mr. Crandall, the hotel manager. Mr. Crandall began to have his own suspicions about Nathan, even though he had been one of their most trusted and well-respected employees. Nevertheless, without alerting Nathan in any way, Mr. Crandall hired an auditor to thoroughly examine the books and report back to him.

The police installed a hidden camera in Nathan's office and set him up with a series of cash transactions to see if he'd take the bait. The auditors combed through the last two years' books and noted the pattern of discrepancies. It was a clever scheme Nathan had constructed, they admitted, but not foolproof. Nathan had obviously become too daring and greedy when he detected certain loopholes in the system. He had exploited them too aggressively and consequently raised too many red flags.

One Monday morning, soon after, Mr. Crandall walked into Nathan's office to confront him and say goodbye. When he heard the news, Nathan was characteristically nonchalant, as if it were a minor matter he could easily clear up. Although he knew he was being cornered, he looked Mr. Crandall straight in the eye.

"Tell you what," Nathan said. "I'm willing to cut you in on a little of the action, if you're interested. No one else has to know. Just between you and me, I can make your life a lot easier. What do you say?"

The hotel manager glared at Nathan in disbelief. "You can't be serious," he said, shaking his head.

"Dead serious, I guarantee you. It's just a numbers game."

Stunned by Nathan's audacity and arrogance, the manager staggered out of the office without another word. The police, waiting in the hallway, quickly moved in and arrested Nathan. They read him his Miranda rights, cuffed him, and led him away to the police car. He did not resist.

At the trial, Nathan was convicted of embezzlement and sentenced to five to ten years in prison. For his crime, the judge added $150,000 in restitution for the funds Nathan had stolen over the course of two years.

Maya decided to file for divorce. She was too ashamed to live in Marquette any longer and moved downstate to start over. They had no kids and few assets to fight over, so it was a clean split.

When Nathan arrived in prison and donned his institutional orange jumpsuit, he seemed to adjust more quickly than he'd expected. Some of the prisoners learned he was a numbers guy and gave him some grudging respect. In their minds, anyone who could figure odds and manipulate numbers was a person who might be very valuable someday. Favors were always in short supply.

Daredevils

In a small town like Sault Ste. Marie (the Soo), there aren't a lot of distractions for guys like me to get all pumped up about, except maybe girls or cars. Sure, there's the usual street dances and dragging the main, if you have wheels, but if you want to have any real fun around here, you have to find your own kicks. My two buddies, Hoagie and Jake, usually come up with something crazy if we wait long enough. So far, I've never been disappointed.

The three of us all plan to take Drivers' Ed. at Soo High this fall. With a driver's license, we can borrow the parents' cars, maybe save up for our own wheels, and start going places. Up till now, we've been depending on our trusty old Schwinn bikes to get around. I know that sounds lame and that's all right, but bicycles aren't exactly chick magnets. It's hard to ask a good-looking girl out on a date with only a three-speed, no matter how cool you look.

What happened to us last week was unbelievable. It's amazing to me how fast things can just spin out of control. I thought we had everything figured out until all hell broke loose. Looking back now, we should have seen it coming. But I'm getting ahead of myself; let me back up a bit.

One sweltering afternoon a week before our senior year of high school started, the three of us—me, Jake, and Hoagie–were floating on our inner-tubes out on Ashmun Bay, near Kemp's coal dock. We had grown tired of pedaling all the way out to Sherman Park, or Ankle Beach as they call it, to check out the babes in bikinis. We had worn that routine out for the summer and wanted some decent water we could actually swim in, not to mention a little peace and quiet. Jake had brought along his flattop guitar and was floating along picking a few tunes and trying to sing. Draped lazily over his inner-tube, Jake seemed so long and skinny, he looked like an over-cooked linguine noodle. The basketball coach had encouraged him to try out for the team because he'd seen him dunk the ball with ease, but Jake didn't want any part of it. He didn't want to be one of the high school jocks–too much of a clique for him. Instead, he preferred pickup street games, good competition without all the hassle of daily practice.

Further out in the St. Mary's River, we could see the big iron-ore freighters coming and going from the Soo Locks. It looked like a romantic way of life, sailing around the Great Lakes from port to port, not a care in the world.

"After I graduate," I said, "I'm going to get my seaman's card and find a decking job on a freighter."

"Yeah, right, Charlie," said Jake. "You wouldn't last a week out there. Don't you realize there are no girls out there except maybe in the galley?"

"Is that right?" I said. "Guess I hadn't thought about that."

He kicked some water at me, but to protect his guitar, I didn't retaliate.

"When I'm finished with school," Jake said, "I might join the Marines, get out of this little hick town, and see the rest of the world. Can't you just see me, jumping out of airplanes, running around the battlefield with my M-1 machine gun, dressed in camouflage? I can hardly wait."

"I wouldn't get so excited about war games if I were you," Hoagie added. "My dad was in the war, and he said it's a lot more brutal and gruesome than you can imagine. Besides, you don't like taking orders from anybody. You'd be in the brig the first month."

It's true. Jake always liked calling the shots and hated anyone telling him what to do. He and his father had butted heads more than a few times in the past. Whether he was looking for trouble or not, it always seemed to find him. Having such a vivid imagination, Jake was just curious about things. The previous couple of summers, he'd gotten on his father's bad side by breaking into someone's cabin in the woods and losing his old man's boat motor in the river. Needless to say, I'm never bored when Jake's around.

"Oh, you're a real smartass," said Jake. "And what are you going to do, work at Burger King for the rest of your life?"

"Real funny," said Hoagie. "At least I've got a summer job and some pocket change. If it weren't for me, you'd have no one to mooch off."

Hoagie did buy us Cokes and burgers once in a while, but we promised to pay him back as soon as we got jobs. He's got a bottomless appetite and can eat more than Jake and I combined, especially when it comes to submarine sandwiches, which is where he got his nickname, Hoagie. He can put away three sub-sandwiches in the time it takes me to eat one Whopper. With barely an effort, he simply inhales them. Built like a lineman, he's very athletic for his size and keeps threatening to join the high school football team, if it doesn't get in the way of his after-school job.

"I'm not sure what to do after high school," Hoagie continued. "I might just work with my dad for a while laying carpet and tile. It pays pretty well."

We rolled off our tubes and swam around in the cool blue water, knowing this might be one of our last chances to hang out together before school resumed. Up to that point, the most exciting thing to happen this summer was watching Neil Armstrong walk on the moon. My brother Jeremy and I, along with my parents, watched that historic first step on our black-and-white Sylvania; the live pictures were a bit fuzzy, but the moment was amazing anyhow.

With so little time left, we wanted to squeeze as much fun and good times out of this final week as possible. We yearned for something adventurous and exciting to highlight our un-remarkable, hot, and boring summer. Something to brag to our friends about over the long stretch of winter.

As good friends ever since grade school, the three of us had done a few wild and crazy things over the years, usually on a dare. One time, we took turns riding down Prospect Hill on our bikes with no hands and at full speed. At the bottom of the hill, two of us held a rope stretched across the road to see if the rider could break through. It seemed like a good idea at the time, but when Jake came speeding down the hill, the rope caught him around the neck. He was unable to hold onto the bike as it slid out from under him. When all was said and done, he burned the hell out of his neck and was picking gravel out of his skin for hours.

Another time, Jake and Hoagie dared me to walk across Ashmun Bridge balanced on the handrail. The bridge, over two-hundred feet in length, stands about thirty feet above the fast-moving power canal that flows beneath it. It was late at night, so there wasn't much traffic and just enough light from the bridge streetlights. Halfway across, my heart was pounding so hard I could barely breathe. Instead of looking straight ahead at the railing as I placed one foot carefully in front of the other, I made the mistake of glancing down at the swift current below me. I tensed up immediately, and my knees buckled. Tumbling onto the sidewalk beside the rails, I must have scared the bejesus out of those guys. They both looked white as ghosts and decided to pass when their turns came.

One of the grossest, most unpleasant things we ever did together was crawling through Ashmun Bridge's overhead structure from one side of the canal to the other. Again, it was late one summer night, with very few people around. When the coast was clear, we climbed inside the hollowed-out grid structure and began our ascent. The bridge arched gracefully over the road, reaching a height of maybe forty feet. A couple of flashlights would have come in really handy at that point. Except for a few dim beams from the streetlights, it was pitch black in there.

As we crawled up to the peak of the span, we could hear a lot of cooing and clucking sounds. Suddenly, we realized we were squirming through mounds of feathers and pigeon guano, probably several years' worth. Who knows what kind of lice, mites, and nameless diseases we were wading through. Since it was no shorter turning around and going back, we pushed on until we reached the other side, inhaling the disgusting stench of rotting pigeon crap. We rousted quite a number of pigeons from the comfort of their roosts that night. I'm sure they were more than a little frightened and confused when they saw strangers crawling through their homestead at such a late hour.

Floating drowsily across Ashmun Bay on our tubes that hot August afternoon, the three of us kicked around ideas for some kind of end-of-summer adventure that would top everything. Something bold and daring. You have to understand a thing or two about Hoagie and Jake. They are usually fearless, acting strictly on instinct. There's not a whole lot they wouldn't do if somebody simply dared them. Both are big-time risk-takers who love living on the edge, and sometimes that scares the hell out of me. So I have to be careful what I ask of them.

"I've got it!" I said, looking east toward the Locks. "You see the power canal way over there? We could take our tubes and float all the way through town."

"That's a really cool idea," said Hoagie, "but that's a pretty strong current in there."

"I've never heard of anyone ever doing anything like that before," said Jake, with a gleam in his eye. "Not in all these years."

The power canal is one thing that makes this small town unique. Starting in Lake Superior, the canal flows over two miles through the middle of town and rejoins the St. Mary's River at the powerhouse, a series of turbines forming a hydroelectric plant. So the water power generates a lot of electricity for city residents and businesses. The only reason I know all this is because last year my history class took a complete tour of the place; it was awesome.

"We're all pretty strong swimmers," I said, "but we'd have to get out before reaching Spruce Street Bridge."

"That current is vicious," said Jake, "but floating through town would be so cool. Never seen it done before."

"You ever wonder why?" I asked. "Haven't you guys ever heard about those turbines at the other end of the canal? If you get sucked into them, your body would be chewed up like you went through a meat grinder."

Hoagie seemed to be having second thoughts, but he didn't want to look like he was chickening out.

"C'mon," said Jake. "Don't be such a pussy! We can do this."

"OK, then," I said, "so we're all in?"

We all slapped high-fives to seal the deal and paddled back to shore to fine-tune our plan. It would have to be top secret; just the three of us would know about it–no other friends and absolutely no parents. If all went well, this stunt would top everything we'd ever done together.

That evening, while Hoagie was working behind the counter, Jake and I hung out at Burger King for a while, throwing down a few Whoppers and Cokes. Our girlfriends, Jasmine and Chloe, happened to stop by and sat down at our booth. When they asked us what we'd been up to, Jake and I glanced at each other and couldn't help but mention our plans for the next day. They suddenly grew very excited.

"You three guys are going to float down the power canal on rubber tubes?" Chloe asked in amazement, as if she misunderstood something. "Why would you do that? Do you have some kind of secret death wish or what?"

Jake shook his head nonchalantly. "No. We just want to have some excitement."

"Well," said Jasmine, "I think it's a really rad idea, even if it is a little whacked."

"Would you girls like to come with us?" I teased.

"Hell, no!" said Chloe. "We might be a little crazy sometimes, but we're not that nuts."

"Please be careful, guys," said Jasmine. "That current looks deadly; might be faster than you think."

"OK," I said, "but keep this quiet. We don't want to tip anyone off."

The next day, near the warmest part of the afternoon, we rode our bikes up to the head of the canal. The lush trees and thick bushes made a perfect place to stash our bikes until later. We stripped down to our swimsuits and went over our last minute plans. We would try to drift toward the south side of the canal, where the current would likely steer us, and stay out of the middle. Six bridges crossed the canal. We would attempt to get out just before the Spruce Street Bridge, the fifth one. It would be the bridge right after Johnstone Street, where the canal starts its bend to the north. There was no point in waiting until the last second to exit.

Hoagie, Jake, and I slapped high-fives and shouted, "Let's do this!"

We pushed off together in our tubes, and the brisk current quickly swept us downstream. It was a beautiful day for a floating trip, and the three of us laughed and joked as the scenery rapidly sped past us. We drifted under the rickety old Fort Street Bridge that was slowly rusting away. The water was chilly but crystal clear, and I wondered how many stolen bikes were lying on the bottom of the canal. There were frequent rumors of thieves stealing bikes, taking them for a joyride, and then dumping the evidence in the canal. I used to daydream about the canal being completely drained dry and walking the length of it searching for lost treasures. Maybe there were bodies, I thought, of people who had mysteriously disappeared. Several suicides had happened in the past from desperate people leaping into the icy waters. Just thinking about it gave me the creeps.

The first few minutes, nobody seemed to notice us floating along. Then as we approached Ashmun Street Bridge, the main downtown crossing, we noticed police cars with their red lights flashing, and long ropes dangling over the bridge railings to the water. As we drifted closer, I caught a glimpse of Chloe and Jasmine standing near several cops. One of them must have tipped off the police at the last minute. They looked determined to save us from certain disaster. A voice from a police bullhorn rang out over the water.

"Gentlemen, what you're doing is totally illegal and very dangerous. Grab a line and we'll get you out!"

Hoagie put both arms over his head in a victory salute and yelled back, "Sorry, officer! Not a chance!"

Jake hollered, "Don't worry about us! We'll be fine!"

We batted the hanging lines out of our way as we drifted past, ignoring their demands. We had too much riding on this trip to abort so early. Shrugging our shoulders, we looked up at everyone and waved like we were in some Fourth of July parade. The bridge was crowded with people leaning over, gawking down at us like aliens from another planet. Someone yelled, "Good luck, guys. You sure got balls!" We smiled back at them but started to wonder what we'd gotten ourselves into.

At Bingham Bridge, another three minutes downstream, there were no dangling ropes, but other police officers yelled down to us to get out at the next bridge before it was too late. Jake and I had drifted a little further downstream than Hoagie, but we tried to paddle over to our right, closer to the south shoreline. Near the next bridge, Johnstone, the canal would swing ninety degrees to the north, so we wanted to be on the outside of that turn. At the water's edge was a series of large timber beams. Above them, hanging slightly over the bank, were clusters of bushes, which we were eyeing up as our means of escape. Johnstone loomed over us suddenly, and again, the police dangled ropes in our faces. We politely ignored them and drifted on. Their threats of arrest seemed meaningless and a little over-the-top, under the circumstances. All we wanted was to float peacefully through town and have a good time. We weren't hurting anybody or damaging any property.

Now, approaching the fifth bridge, Spruce Street, it was time to make our move. The three of us paddled close to the outside bank, the centrifugal force pushing us in that direction. Jake made a grab for a hanging branch, but it slipped from his hands. Finally, I reached for a branch and struggled in the current to pull myself out. I had underestimated the swiftness of the force under me and lost my tube in the current. Jake soon found a solid overhanging branch and fought his way out. Twenty yards behind us, Hoagie neared the bank and yanked several branches out by their roots as he sped by.

"C'mon, Hoagie! Grab on!" we yelled.

He drifted past us and tried again. On his third attempt, he pulled the overhanging branch with such force that his tube shot out from under him, and he was suddenly thrashing around in the current, floating away from the bank.

"Help me, guys! Help me!" he shouted.

"Hang on, Hoagie! Swim!"

We could see the Spruce Street Bridge but no dangling ropes for Hoagie to grab. We knew he was a strong swimmer, but that current was a powerful force, much stronger than we had thought possible.

Jake and I climbed up the canal bank and over the fence, but before we could escape, a squad car pulled over to pick us up. When we told them Hoagie was still in the water, drifting closer to the powerhouse turbines, the cops quickly drove us down to the Portage Street Bridge, the last one before the meat grinder.

Minutes before we arrived on the scene, Hoagie had come floating under the Portage Bridge, and this time he had latched onto one of the dangling ropes the cops had dropped and hung on for dear life. They reeled him in near the shoreline, not fifty yards from the powerhouse's churning underbelly. Hoagie was exhausted by the whole ordeal, but alive and well.

A crowd had gathered near the Portage Bridge while Hoagie was being hauled out of the drink. As we ran to the railing to see what was happening, we overheard a few comments: "Cocky little bastards. Who do they think they are? Ferris Bueller?" *The Evening News* photographers were there snapping pictures of us and asking all kinds of questions: "What made you boys do this? What were you trying to accomplish?"

Next day, our pictures were splashed across the front page of *The Evening News* under the caption, "Last Hurrah Before School?" The three of us were hauled into juvenile court with our parents, who grounded us for two months. The court penalized us with sixty days of litter-pickup on the city streets, but nothing permanent on our records.

I guess you could say we made the history books, at least on a local level. And best of all, the chicks loved it; that's all they talked about during our first week of school. For months, we had some serious swag and great reps. On the other hand, it could have been much worse. We were so lucky to come out of this escapade in one piece. The hard part now is figuring out how to top this escapade next summer. I wouldn't mind buying a chopper, even one of those nasty crotch-rockets. That would open up a whole new world of possibility, especially in a town like this.

The Craftsman

Michael first met Samantha at Art on the Rocks, Marquette's annual summer art show. Her canopy of landscape paintings and marine art was set up next to his woodworking and furniture pieces. When a sudden wind gust blew in off Lake Superior, her paintings began to topple from their tripods, and her fragile canopy nearly went airborne. Michael had weighted all the corners of his setup with fifty-pound cement blocks, but it looked like Samantha was new to the art fair circuit. Apparently, she hadn't anticipated any inclement weather. Michael grabbed one corner of her canopy and held the post down in the wind while she steadied the opposite corner, waiting for the storm to subside.

Within a few minutes, the wind quieted down, and the sun reappeared from behind the clouds. They picked the paintings off the ground, brushed them off, and remounted them on their easels. Luckily, there was no serious damage.

"Well, that was a close call," said Michael. "You need some weights on these corners or you'll lose it all."

"Thanks for your help," she said, squinting at him through her dark sunglasses. "My name's Samantha."

She thrust her hand toward him, and they shook. He noticed her tie-dyed long skirt and her jet-black hair tied back in a ponytail. "Hi, I'm Michael. Are you new to these art fairs, or do you just like living dangerously?"

"It's not my first rodeo, but it's my first summer doing this. So far I've had good weather; this is only my third outdoor show."

"Well, you've been lucky. You can never count on good weather on the circuit. Have to be ready for the worst—my philosophy of life."

Samantha smiled back at Michael and said, "I don't believe in luck, but I do believe in practicing good karma. We receive from the world in proportion to what we give."

Michael liked her friendly, easy-going manner and asked her out for dinner after the show. They stopped by the Villa Capri for some Italian food. It was his favorite restaurant whenever he booked a show in Marquette—a relaxing atmosphere and great cuisine at a fair price. When the bread and salad arrived, they toasted the end of a long day with a glass of red wine.

Samantha lifted her glass and said, "Here's to starving artists everywhere. May they earn enough to pay their bills and pursue their art."

"Here, here," said Michael, "and may they save enough for the proverbial rainy day."

Michael had had a fairly successful day at the art fair, selling a rocking chair, several Swedish door harps, a couple of jewelry boxes, and some cutting boards. He greatly disliked building so-called bread-and-butter pieces like cutting boards and birdhouses, but they helped to pay the bills. If he had his way, he would design and build nothing but one-of-a-kind furniture with a sculptural flair. But he realized he might slowly starve because one-of-a-kind work was very pricey and did not move as quickly as less expensive pieces. So, for him, it was always a compromise between the ideal and the practical.

On the other hand, Samantha had sold only one painting all day, a landscape of the Sleeping Bear Dunes, for $375. Most of her paintings were priced in a similar range. However, during the day, she had talked with quite a number of very interested customers who had praised her work, so she felt good about the day overall.

"I handed out oodles of business cards today," said Samantha. "I'm hoping I can stir up a commission or two. It's getting expensive to run around to all these art fairs."

"You're telling me. After the entry fees, hotels, food, and gas, there's not a whole lot left."

"Maybe you do this mostly for the sheer love of it, the lifestyle," she said.

Michael laughed. "That's right. I love the wind and the rain, the hot, muggy weather, traveling all summer like a gypsy, and, of course, the solitude of working alone. I must be a masochist."

Samantha smiled. "I know what you mean, but compared to other options, I'd much rather spend my time painting sailboats on west Grand Traverse Bay or lighthouses around Michigan than clerking at Walmart. It takes a lot of discipline to keep working by yourself, to be productive, but I think it's worthwhile. I just hope I can scratch out a living at this."

"That's the great conundrum. What starts as a romantic ideal quickly becomes a gritty, practical business. There's no other way. It's like being doomed to follow your dreams. Thank God for wine and whiskey at the end of the day."

When the spaghetti and meatballs arrived, they both ate with hearty appetites and talked about life on the art fair circuit. It was fairly new and exciting to Samantha, having studied painting for two years at Northwestern Michigan

College (NMC) in Traverse City (TC). Although she was living with her parents in Suttons Bay, she yearned to have her own studio soon and be independent. She hoped to build up a clientele through her contacts at art fairs and galleries around the state.

During the long Michigan winters, Michael worked in his shop just west of Traverse City, building up his inventory for the summer season. His furniture design degree from Northern Michigan University in Marquette had come in handy, inspiring him to design furniture that had a sculptural flow to it. He built maple stools, cherry cabinets, and walnut tables with sliding dovetails and pinned mortise-tenon joints. He loved the smell of freshly planed wood shavings in his shop. Fortunately, Michael was disciplined enough to work by himself and still be productive every day. There was no one to push him but himself. And he preferred it that way.

The winter hours were long and sometimes lonely for him. He often wished he could share his love for art and wood-working with a kindred soul. When he first met Samantha, he seemed to have a fresh spring in his step. She occupied his thoughts throughout the day. Would two artists with different artistic interests ever make a good team? he wondered. Or was having too much in common impractical? She was very talented, he realized, as well as very beautiful. And, in Suttons Bay, she virtually lived in his backyard. As Samantha might say, it was just good karma.

Between fairs, Michael was back in TC for a few days. Whenever he could, he called Samantha to go out for coffee or drinks. It wasn't until the third date that he tried to kiss her. They had been walking along the marina and the beach one evening in Suttons Bay. Saying goodnight at her doorstep and hugging her closely, he picked up the unmistakable scent of her perfume. Patchouli, he guessed. He gave her a long kiss and told her he'd had a great evening. She pulled him in close, shut her eyes, and returned the kiss.

The next morning, they would be heading to art fairs in opposite directions. She was driving north to the Soo, and he was booked in Ann Arbor for the weekend. Marquette had been the only show they would have in common all summer.

The first day for Michael fizzled out. It rained steadily in Ann Arbor most of the day, so patrons stayed dry inside at the coffee shops and restaurants. But the sun came back out the second day, and business was brisk.

Samantha had a better than usual day in the Soo. She sold a $450 painting of the Chicago-to-Mackinac sailboat race and lined up a commission to paint the historic Chippewa County Courthouse. The wind and rain retreated for the weekend and made life considerably more pleasant.

By late August, Michael had finished up his last few shows in Petoskey, Bay City, and Grand Rapids. Just as well since he was running quite low on inventory and the trailer he pulled behind his pickup was in need of a new coat of paint and a set of tires. He was ready to enjoy the relaxing days of September before getting back to full-time work in his shop. Besides, he would have more time to spend with Samantha, who had signed up to take a couple of classes at NMC in philosophy and American folklore.

Since Samantha lived at home, her parents began to wonder about the man in her life and the long late-night phone conversations. So Michael finally introduced himself when he was invited over one night for dinner. They asked curiously about his career goals and prospects, and he replied honestly. Making a living as a full-time artist was very fulfilling, but it was a year-to-year struggle. Some years were good, some more challenging.

When the season ended every year, Michael liked to assess the good and the bad, which pieces had sold well and which had flopped. Did any prices need to be tweaked? He thought about designing a few new pieces over the winter, possibly incorporating stained glass with some of his cabinets and jewelry boxes. To give Samantha's paintings a more custom look, he offered to create some wooden frames. In return, she agreed to paint some better signage for his booth.

To save expenses, Michael bought green lumber from a local sawmill and air-dried it himself. He inventoried his wood supply and ordered more cherry and walnut, which would be used mostly for Swedish door harps and jewelry boxes. He had learned to price his work as accurately as possible. Although it was more complex than he had first realized, the prices had to be affordable or they would never sell. He had to take into account not only his labor, the saws and sanders, and various hand tools in his shop, but also electricity costs, lumber, art fair entry fees, self-employment taxes, and travel costs.

When Michael read back through the pages of his comments book, which he had always made available for customers to sign, he felt vindicated in his choice of work. *"Great Work!"* *"You have a vivid imagination and a skillful touch!"* *"Beautiful Woodwork!"* So many people seemed to appreciate his craftsmanship and the quality of his designs. The individuality of the work and the customers' response was pay in itself.

Michael imagined other artists probably made more money than him—especially the jewelers, potters, and photographers. There always seemed to be crowds around those particular booths. But working wood was a slow medium and a time-consuming process. For Michael, despite its drawbacks, the bottom line was: He loved his independence. He called all the shots, and he made all the decisions. He knew the risks and often felt the adrenaline rush of running such a business, but he felt it was the only life for him.

Over the winter months, Samantha spent much of her time painting from photographs she had taken of local scenes—ice fishermen on the bay, lighthouses blasted by the latest winter blizzard, vineyards on the Old Mission peninsula. She liked to use photos as a starting point and add other details as she went along.

Samantha and Michael spent many hours together having coffee, at the theater, and just walking about town discussing art and their future prospects. He invited her out to his farmhouse for dinner and to show her his shop and the old barn he used for drying lumber. He was renting the property for a reasonable price from an out-of-town landlord with one stipulation: he would do his own repairs whenever necessary. Since he couldn't afford to buy any property yet, it was a good arrangement. Going out for dinner often in TC was too expensive for his budget, so he did most of his own cooking.

To help pay the bills all winter, Michael found it necessary to work a part-time job at a local Ace Hardware store. He offered customers advice on building projects, furniture repair, and interior painting. Between shoveling snow and miscellaneous housework, there wasn't a great deal of time left for design work and furniture building. He had to use his free time wisely to prepare for the upcoming art fair season.

After Christmas, Samantha found a small apartment on Union Street, above a drugstore. It had large, sunny bay windows that brightened the rooms, and the bedroom doubled as a studio. It didn't allow her much space to spread out, but it provided her independence from her parents' home. To help afford it, she placed some of her paintings in local art galleries on a consignment basis. They usually charged her a 30 percent commission and paid her the balance. She soon picked up a part-time waitressing job at the North Peak, a pub/restaurant in TC that served burgers, pizza, and a selection of proprietary IPA. By saving her tips and carefully budgeting her expenses, Samantha managed to keep up with her bills every month. She hoped someday money wouldn't be such a problem.

Surviving as an artist was not always the romantic lifestyle she had imagined. She would try another year on the art fair circuit to see if her situation improved. *Maybe,* she thought, *I'm not cut out to be this struggling artist. Maybe I need to move on to something more practical.*

By late April, about a month before the new season started up, both Michael and Samantha were working diligently, building up their inventories and setting up their show schedules. One evening, they met for happy hour at a downtown bar for a few beers and to catch up on each other's very busy life. Samantha had been having a rather hectic day and was not in a particularly good mood.

"This place kind of sucks," she said. "The drinks are way too expensive, even at happy hour prices. Why'd we have to come here?"

"Whoa, you're in rare form. What's up with you tonight?" Michael asked.

Samantha wouldn't look at him but stared down at her drink as if in a daze. "I'm moving back home next month."

"What?" Michael asked. "Are you serious?"

"I pay my rent and utilities, buy my food and gas, and at the end of the month, there's nothing left. I can't even afford to buy any new clothes. It's been over five years since I took a decent vacation."

Michael took a long look at her, thinking of how she'd been raised as an only child, as the focus of her parents' eyes for more than two decades. "You're a bit spoiled," he said, "and you don't even realize it. You are twenty-five years old; you can't move back in with your parents. You need your independence. My old man told me that once I moved out, I could never come back, except for a visit. You don't really want to do that."

"What's the point of working all day and giving it all away again for bills? At home, I didn't have to worry about those things. I just took care of myself and my own personal expenses."

Michael gave her a sly, incredulous smile. "Your parents have been paying your expenses for several years—your room and board, your clothes, your car insurance. You're acting like a spoiled little brat who can't save a penny. You just don't know any better, I guess."

Samantha jumped up from the table and slammed her beer down. "That's enough of this! I don't have to listen to this crap. You know what? We are through. I should've known that two starving artists could never make it together. It's not possible. You will be poor for the rest of your life, but I don't want any part of it. I am out of here."

She grabbed her purse and headed for the door, then looked back at him and said, "And don't bother calling me ever again."

At home that night, Michael built a fire in the woodstove to ease the chill in the air. Staring at the crackling flames, he wondered if he had been too hard on her, too honest for his own good. But she *was* spoiled, he thought, or maybe pampered was a better word. She wanted her parents to care for her like she was a child without any responsibility. But why, he asked himself, did he have to point out the obvious? Couldn't he have been more tactful, more diplomatic, instead of speaking so bluntly, so straight-forwardly? That occasionally got him into trouble with his friends. In many situations, he felt a need to be brutally honest with people, even if they misunderstood him at times. There was not enough subtlety, no hinting around—just a bare-knuckles gut reaction to things. Until now, Michael hadn't realized his approach could be so hurtful.

Meanwhile, Samantha was wounded by Michael's words and tone. He had never spoken to her like that before. In some ways, she thought, maybe he was right. She had never really had to stand on her own two feet before, at least not for very long because her parents always bailed her out. They had the money, and she didn't. Simple as that. Nevertheless, she did not appreciate being called *spoiled*. Despite how she missed Michael as the days passed, she refused to call him back.

Instead of moving back home with her parents in Suttons Bay, Samantha moved into a three-bedroom house with a couple of girlfriends. Since this new arrangement saved both time and expenses, she was able to help out more with the house-cleaning and meals.

Finally, the art fair season was in full swing, and both Michael and Samantha were on the run every weekend to shows around the state. They crossed paths in Marquette and again in Petoskey, said hello, but awkwardly avoided each other. Regardless, Michael admired the professional-looking signs Samantha had painted for his booth, and she appreciated the finely crafted oak-and-cherry frames he had built to enhance her paintings.

There was a void in their lives that neither was willing to admit. Maybe the time away from each other was good in some ways for their relationship. Michael missed Samantha's quirkiness and the way she laughed at things he said. He missed holding her and running his fingers through her long black hair. She missed his arms around her, his kiss, and the way he smiled at her when she talked passionately about her painting. But neither of them wanted to make the first move.

On his way home from a show in Bay City, Michael finally reached the end of his rope. This pig-headedness, he decided, had gone on long enough. He pulled over to the side of the road and called Samantha on his cell. When she answered, it was such a relief to hear her voice.

"Sam, I am so sorry for the way I treated you. I didn't mean to hurt you intentionally. Do you think we could get together and try things again?"

There was a long pause and some quiet sniffling on her end of the line while she took a deep breath and tried to compose herself. "I thought you'd given up on me . . . or found someone else . . . ."

"I would never do that," he said.

"I've missed you terribly all summer, wondering where you were and what you were thinking. My life feels so empty without you."

"I want to make it up to you. I'll be back home in a few hours. Can we go out to dinner tonight at our favorite restaurant?"

They celebrated their reunion that evening at Boone's Long Lake Inn with a dinner of steak and shrimp and a bottle of cabernet sauvignon. It was a rare occasion for them to splurge, but their anticipation of a new beginning demanded nothing less.

Since the art fair season was quickly winding down, Samantha and Michael exchanged stories of their show experiences. After the setting up and tearing down, the unpredictable weather, the long drives and so forth, life on the road had become a grind for both of them. Michael suggested a possible solution.

"Here's an idea I've been considering for a while. It's a gamble, but it might be worth it in the long run," he said.

"Let's hear it."

"OK, I propose that you and I set up our own art gallery in TC. I know of a warehouse space not far from downtown that we could convert into a gallery for our work and for a few other select artists. We could staff it ourselves for a while to avoid employee costs and maybe do some of our own work there. We would give up the art fair circuit completely except for three or four of the best shows, and we would share space and expenses traveling back and forth. What do you say?"

"It sounds very exciting. The constant traveling has been wearing me down. Maybe we both need a fresh start."

"We can set up our own website and promote our work more on the internet. And the best part—we'll have more time for each other."

Samantha and Michael both raised a glass to toast their new relationship and their budding business venture. The days ahead would be filled with renovations, business details, and plans for the grand opening of their new gallery. Despite the anxiety and fretfulness of undertaking a new enterprise, their ambition rekindled a fire within them. What was good for their souls and artistic growth, they believed, would also be good for them. A finely crafted life, in the long run, just might be worth the gamble.

The Bargain Hunter

"Going once! Going twice . . . ! Sold to the young lady in the corner!"

The auctioneer banged his gavel on the makeshift desk, and his helpers gathered the boxes of miscellaneous treasures and delivered them to Serena in the corner of the auction barn. So far this evening, she had been the highest bidder for a set of twelve pink champagne glasses, four orange life jackets, a small chest of drawers, and a set of law books. She had wanted to bid on a brass bed and a mahogany bookcase, but she wasn't sure they would all fit into her Chrysler Caravan, a ten-year-old clunker that was having serious issues with its springs and shocks.

When the weekly auction ended, Serena loaded up her goods and drove back to her small farmhouse just a few miles south of Sault Ste. Marie. In her divorce ten years earlier, she had ended up with the farmhouse and a small pole barn, which had come in handy for storing her accumulated treasures. She had a discerning eye for a bargain and pursued it like a hunter pursues game, mostly for the sport, but also because a good deal was often too irresistible to pass up.

To Serena, bargain-hunting was a calling. She saw glowing possibilities where others saw absolute junk. She saw utility and practicality where others saw mounting clutter. In Serena's eyes, every object might someday occupy a very special place in one of her farmhouse rooms. Otherwise, her newly-acquired treasures could find a temporary home in her old jelly cabinet, a cache of gifts for upcoming birthdays and special occasions. It was just a matter of bold vision and creativity. She thought perhaps she might one day set up her own bed-and-breakfast rental on Airbnb if she could decorate the rooms in a striking way and clean out some of the unnecessary clutter.

The next morning, Serena rose bright and early and was off to see her first client. She grabbed a cup of coffee and her lipstick on the way out the door, quickly brushing her hair as she went. Halfway through her forties, she still considered herself reasonably attractive but did not spend a great deal of time preening or dressing.

Serena regretted having married several months out of high school; she'd thought she was head over heels in love with a boy. Although her marriage didn't last for more than a few years, she was proud of herself for having raised two fine sons who had turned into respectable and caring young men. After her divorce, she had started a small business cleaning homes and apartments. Self-employment had restored her sense of dignity and self-respect and allowed her to set her own hours. Serena had built up a loyal following and was in great demand for several reasons. She not only cleaned rooms but was also able to do minor home repairs like patching drywall, fixing leaky faucets, wall-papering, and setting tiles. With such a busy workload, she had no problem staying in good physical shape and felt no need even to consider joining a gym.

Over the years, many of Serena's clients offered her furniture or household items they wanted to clear out. Usually a chair leg needed gluing or a drawer needed repair of some kind. She rarely refused the offer if the items could fit into her van. On days off, Serena regularly shopped Goodwill and the Salvation Army to see if any bargains had cropped up. She was seldom disappointed. On Friday and Saturday mornings during the summer months, she hit the neighborhood garage sales around town, negotiating deals on everything from lamps and tables that needed a little fixing to name-brand, stainless steel cookware and collections of *National Geographic* from the '60s and '70s. The set of law books she had scored from the auction, she felt, might come in handy if she pursued her pipedream of becoming a lawyer. Her assortment of medical dictionaries and textbooks would serve her well someday when she resumed her nursing education. Even her collection of woodworking tools and home repair manuals might be just the thing when she became one of the few female carpenters in the U.P. The way Serena saw things, one could never be too prepared for whatever was around the next corner.

One Saturday evening, Serena was getting dressed up to attend a bluegrass concert at the college fine arts building. Her on-again, off-again boyfriend, Carl, was due to pick her up at 7:30 p.m., but he pulled his car up to the house ten minutes early. When he stepped up to the front porch, she met him at the door.

"I'm a bit early," he said, "but I can come in and wait if you're not quite ready."

"That's OK," she said, smiling coyly, "I'll just brush my hair and meet you in the car. Be there in just a minute."

"Oh, there's no rush. I'll just come in and sit down."

"Well, I don't want to be late for the show. I'll be right out."

She waved him off and closed the door, dodging the tall piles of boxes in the hallway on her way to the kitchen. There wouldn't have been a place for Carl to sit anyway, she thought. Her sofa and living room chairs had disappeared long ago under piles of books and magazines. Plastic bins of clothes and cleaning supplies had been stacked in the dining room and on the steps leading upstairs. There was a narrow pathway zigzagging between the heaps of household treasures. A large-screen TV could barely be seen in the far corner of the room; it hadn't been switched on for months.

For someone living on such a tight budget, Serena dressed fairly well. She mixed her skirts, blouses, and high heels with a unique flair her girlfriends envied. They always noticed she had a good eye for creative styling. Most of her clothes had come from garage sales and secondhand stores, but they were of very high quality. Her wardrobe was spread over three closets, four chests of drawers, and a number of miscellaneous boxes.

Serena walked back through the kitchen to check the lock on the back door. The floor and kitchen counters were crammed with canned goods and boxes of Special K, Cheerios, and Wheaties. There had been a recent sale at Walmart on tuna fish, and she had purchased twenty-five cans at every visit, thinking they would keep well. Dish detergent was a bargain at The Dollar Store, so Serena had stocked up on that as well. The stack of dirty dishes near the sink was expanding because she had run out of time trying to keep up with them. Instead, she covered the pile with old newspapers so she wouldn't have to be reminded of them.

Carl beeped his horn out front, and Serena hurried down the cluttered hallway and out the door. Due to the circumstances, she was much too embarrassed to invite Carl or any of her friends into her house. She had every intention of cleaning it up, of rearranging things, but she always ran out of time. She worked many long and exhausting hours keeping her clients' homes spotless, but she felt overwhelmed when she came home at the end of the day.

How Serena had ever managed to raise her two boys, Josh

and Luke, was a miracle to her, and she was rightfully proud. For years, she had pushed them both through college until they had finally graduated. Soon Josh had settled down as a high school teacher in town, and Luke worked as a retail store manager. Once a month, they took her out for Sunday dinner at the casino or for a fish-fry in Brimley.

For several years, the boys had said nothing about their mother's hoarding issues. They figured she would simply tire of the overwhelming clutter someday and clean it out once and for all. Over the years, Serena had gradually stopped allowing anyone else in her house, friends and neighbors included. She had not invited anyone over for drinks or conversation in a long time. Her social life was of no great importance to her anymore. Because of the stacked up piles of clutter in the utility room, Serena could no longer make her way to the washer and dryer, so her social life now consisted of frequent trips to the laundromat.

The boys could both sense their mother's mood had changed. She wasn't necessarily depressed, but neither was she her usual upbeat, carefree self. One evening, while Serena was finishing off her McDonald's hamburger and fries, there was a knock on her front door. In walked Josh and Luke for a surprise visit. After the usual hugs and greetings, the boys got right to the point.

"Mom, we've been meaning to talk to you about your situation for quite some time," said Luke.

"Oh? What situation is that?" asked Serena with a look of surprise.

"The piles of stuff, the clutter everywhere, Mom. You've become a first-class hoarder. Doesn't this bother you at all?"

"It's really no concern of yours, boys. I'm perfectly happy with things the way they are," said Serena. "Would you like something to drink?"

"What we'd really like," said Josh, "is to help you clean out these rooms one by one."

Feeling somewhat cornered, Serena jumped up from her chair and walked out to the kitchen for a cup of coffee. The boys followed her, hoping somehow to persuade her.

"This is my personal business," she said, pointing her finger at them, "and I don't need either of you butting in. I know you mean well, but surely, you have something better to do."

The boys looked at each other, realizing this was going to be much more difficult than anticipated.

In exasperation, Luke said, "Why don't you let us help you? We can give this stuff away or have a huge yard sale. This place is a terrible fire hazard, and we're worried about you."

"Boys, I'm saving a lot of this stuff for you, when you both buy your first houses. I've got all kinds of dishes, small kitchen appliances, lamps, and other things that will get you started, save you money."

"Thanks, Mom, but we really don't want any of it. We like to shop for our own needs."

"But these are all first-rate, name-brand items. You'll see."

"We don't want it! Any of it!" said Josh, grabbing his mother by the shoulders to get his point across. "You've got to stop living like this. Can't you see you're living in a fire trap?"

Serena dropped her head down in her lap and sobbed quietly. Her face reddened as she closed her eyes. Luke put his arms around her and said, "Mom, we only want what's best for you. But we can't let you live like this. You raised us to care about people and to do what's right. Well, this is just not right."

For now, the boys did not want to push her any harder. She had felt hurt by their interference and needed time to recover. They could talk again at another time, she agreed. At the very least, the boys had planted a seed that might take root.

Although Serena was alone many evenings, she was seldom lonely. She kept busy reading mysteries and romance novels, talking to friends on the phone, and catching up with her letter writing to friends who had moved away. On some nights, she took self-defense classes or signed up for a seminar on home-building skills. Without a husband around to help out, she would have to be the jack-of-all-trades. Nevertheless, Serena enjoyed her solitude almost as a luxury. It enabled her to unwind after a tiring day of painting, wall-papering, or cleaning toilets. A good book and a glass of cabernet were sometimes all she needed to relax.

What really made Serena's heart race was a live auction or an estate sale. Perhaps it was the thrill of the hunt, the intense chase for something beautiful and desirable that quickened her pulse. It might be an elegant stained-glass table lamp or simply a crystal paperweight, and she would be one of two late bidders who had persisted to the end. She would subtly nod her approval every time the auctioneer asked for a higher bid until he finally banged the gavel and announced, "Sold!" It was pure ecstasy to have survived the hunt and bagged her coveted quarry. The item she bid on was never something she absolutely needed at that moment, but rather something she absolutely wanted. Serena loved deciding things in the heat of the moment. The excitement of the transaction made her feel good about herself, as if she had attained some elusive goal.

Many of Serena's friends had hobbies, like dancing or gardening. This was her hobby, bargain-hunting, always trying to find a diamond in the rough. At first, her obsession was no big deal. But as her small pole barn and most of the rooms in her house began to fill to capacity, other people started to notice. Why, she wondered, should others complain about her hobby? It was her own personal business as far as she was concerned. What she really needed, she thought, was a larger house and maybe a few new, less nosey, friends.

On Friday morning, Serena finished her coffee and toast with raspberry jam and looked over her list of cleaning jobs for the day. She had three jobs lined up in town that would take her until about four o'clock, if the day went well. On her drive into town, she ran across two garage sales and found a small juicer and a popcorn air popper she couldn't live without; she negotiated a better price by purchasing both items. They would make a nice addition to her collection of small kitchen appliances.

When Serena arrived in town, she went straight to work. Her morning of vacuuming, dusting, and washing clothes seemed to pass quickly, and soon she was on to her next client's home. Then her cellphone went off, a call from her girlfriend, Wanda, who was frantic and could hardly speak.

"Serena! Oh, my God! Your house is on fire! Thank God you're not in it. I heard it on my police scanner and drove there to make sure."

"No, no! My house? Are you sure? This can't be." Then Serena remembered the coffeepot she'd forgotten to unplug. She burst into tears, stepped on the gas, and raced toward the blaze. She had heard several fire-truck sirens a few minutes earlier but had ignored them. When she arrived on the scene, police were attempting to hold back onlookers and TV news people with their cameras. The entire farmhouse was engulfed in flames, and no possibility existed of saving the structure. Serena stared sadly at the inferno as it consumed every possession she owned, years of lovingly acquired treasures, bargains she had discovered and spent her hard-earned money on. She was almost too numb to cry and merely leaned against a wooden fence and watched as the flames quickly consumed her past.

At first, Serena wondered if someone had set the fire intentionally. Was somebody trying to get back at her or teach her a lesson? Who would do such a thing? Then she remembered her boys' admonition that the place was a fire trap.

Two hours later, when the blaze had been thoroughly extinguished, Serena spoke to the fire marshal. From all indications, he believed the fire had started in the kitchen, mostly from an overloaded circuit. She remembered her microwave, toaster, and coffeepot had all been plugged into one outlet, the one nearest the kitchen table.

The small pole barn and all its contents had survived, but Serena's photographs and family albums of her boys growing up had all been destroyed. They had been stored in a living room bookcase inside the farmhouse. Serena felt as if her precious memories had been permanently incinerated, her links to the past irrevocably severed.

For several weeks afterward, Serena was stunned, as if in a daze and unsure what to do next. She had difficulty concentrating on work and everyday tasks. Many of her friends and clients stepped forward to offer her a place to stay until she could get back on her feet. Her home insurance covered the loss of the structure and a certain percentage for typical household furniture and possessions. But it could never reimburse her for the money and effort she had wrapped up in her personal valuables. To her, they were priceless–years of hard work gone up in smoke.

Within a few months, Serena decided to sell her property and auction off the contents of her pole barn. Her sons and friends encouraged her to start fresh, to put the burden behind her. On the one hand, she felt scarred from the fire, having lost everything she held so dear. But at the same time, she sensed a freedom and independence that had been missing for years. If she could somehow get past this overwhelming personal loss, it would be a perfect opportunity to reinvent herself. Serena had underestimated the strain and responsibility of caring for such a massive collection of possessions over the years. Now, suddenly, it was all gone. The numbing reality of it all took some time to sink in.

Serena rented a small apartment overlooking the lower St. Mary's River. Every morning, the sun filled her waterfront windows with views of sailboats and freighters passing in the river. She had decided to cut back on her work schedule and use some of her insurance settlement to pay for her return to college. Despite her mature age, she would pursue her nursing degree again and try to stay on track.

It was difficult to drive past garage sales and the Goodwill store, but she had changed course and wanted to leave her old life behind. In her hands, Serena often held the crystal paperweight she had rescued from the fire's ashes. She clasped it tightly to her breast and thought of the promise she had made to herself. Once it was cleaned up and polished, its crystal brilliance sparkled.

Slam Dunk

Last season, our high school varsity basketball team, the Mapleton Mavericks, lost every single game we played, 0 for 22. You'd think the whole team would be totally demoralized after a year like that, but we weren't. In fact, we were kind of proud of ourselves, in a badass sort of way. Let me explain.

I've been playing hoops since grade school, with a lot of the same guys. By the time we got to high school, most of us had grown quite a bit taller and put on a few more pounds. To make varsity, the coaches encouraged us to work out in the weight room during the off season and put in some court time working on our shots. Playing with one another for so long, we had gotten to know each other's moves, both strengths and weaknesses. That comes in handy during a game, believe me.

My senior year at Mapleton, I made varsity again, as a point guard. I'm only 5' 10", so I have to hustle down the court to avoid any defensive traps. Still, I can get above the rim and dunk when I have to. My best friends on the team, Steve Jenkins and Larry Madigan, are also seniors. Steve is our center, our biggest guy on the team at 6' 4"; he's slightly overweight, but a beast under the backboard. We call him "Mo," short for molasses, because he moves so slowly down the court. He's our best rebounder and is always good for a short layup if we can get the ball to him inside. Larry plays the forward position and is one of our most dependable players, which is how he earned his nickname "Money." When it comes down to crunch time, we can usually count on his shot going down. I go by Tommy, but most of my friends call me "T," short for Turbo since I race up and down the court on all cylinders. I'm a lot like the Pistons' Rick Hamilton a few years ago, always in motion, trying to wear down the defense.

We had a new coach that year, Tom Connors, a P.E. teacher from downstate. At first, he seemed like a real "Xs and Os" kind of guy, who liked to work out offensive strategies on paper and then execute them. At the start of the season, Coach Connors wasn't exactly unfriendly, but you knew right off he would never be close to you as a player. He was a strict disciplinarian, almost military-like in the way he coached. We learned later that Coach had served two tours of duty in the Iraq War and, consequently, expected to run the team like a tight ship. As we ran our wind sprints and practice drills, he barked at us like a Marine sergeant.

"Jenkins, move your fat ass down the floor! Faster, faster! That's better."

He'd blow the whistle in the middle of our lay-up drills. "Madigan, you've missed two lay-ups! My ninety-year-old grandmother can shoot better than that, and she's half-blind and crippled."

In the middle of one practice, he zeroed in on me. "Barnes, for God's sake, you're racing up and down the court like a nervous jack rabbit! Do you have any idea what play we just called or defensive set we're supposed to be in? No, I didn't think so."

Our first game of the season was against Newberry, about an hour's drive from town. We stayed close to them the entire game but mishandled the ball near the end and lost by two points.

Three days later, we were up against Brimley, a team we

had beaten regularly in the past. Again we traded buckets with them most of the game, even had the lead several times, then missed a couple of crucial free throws at the wire and crashed.

For the next few practices, we worked hard on passing drills and free throws. Coach Connors even had players yelling at the shooter, trying to distract and pressure him, to simulate a real game situation.

Over the next several weeks, we lost four straight games to Pickford, Alpena, Gaylord, and St. Ignace. One was right to the wire; the other three were blowouts. It was a long, quiet ride home on the bus those nights. At 0-6, we were starting to doubt ourselves. Coach Connors shuffled the lineup a little, tried new plays and defensive sets, but nothing seemed to work well.

Marquette came to town one Friday night, and at halftime, we were trailing by fifteen points. We stumbled back to our locker room at halftime, feeling humiliated and overmatched. Coach slammed the door behind us. His face was beet red with sweat, and he glared at each of us like we'd committed a crime.

"Son of a bitch! Is that the best you guys can do? That team is pissing all over you, and you don't seem to care." He threw his clipboard across the room at the empty lockers. "You're all playing like a bunch of pussies out there! Where's the effort? Where's the pride? I'm ashamed to even be your coach."

Most of the players refused to look up at him. They hung their heads between their knees and stared at the floor. No one breathed a word. We were shell-shocked and embarrassed, but nobody was ready to throw in the towel.

During the second half, we definitely showed a spark that wasn't there before. We hustled for every loose ball and played aggressive defense, but Marquette had a couple of hot shooters we couldn't seem to stop. Halfway through the fourth quarter, three of us fouled out, mostly from reach-in and blocking fouls. But down the stretch, we caved again, missing two easy lay-ups and several crucial free throws, and came out on the short end. Coach looked like he'd blown a gasket and wouldn't even talk to us after the game. We showered in silence, dressed, and went home. We were now 0 and 11 at the midpoint of our season. As the slaughter continued, surprisingly, not a single player was willing to give up or quit the team in disgust. Everyone just hung in there.

At after-school practice, Coach drilled us mercilessly on specific plays: 2-1-2 and 1-3-1 defensive sets and press breaks. As point guard, I usually brought the ball down the court and, admittedly, was guilty of turning the ball over a number of times when the other team pressed us on the inbound pass. Whenever they double-team you, someone needs to come back quickly to help out. You've got only ten seconds to get the ball over the half-court line, but you can't panic. So we worked hard on press breaks and keeping cool under pressure.

During one of our team scrimmages, I was getting frustrated. Coach Connors insisted on us following specific offensive plays, no matter what. When the play broke down due to a superior defense, we were supposed to execute it anyway. At one point, I looked over at the coach and raised my hand. Coach yelled across the gym.

"Whatsa matter, Barnes? Are you hurt or just giving up?"

"No, sir. I know how to fix this. If a play isn't working, we need to improvise a little, freestyle, you know."

Coach strolled slowly across the floor toward me. "Are you challenging me, Barnes?"

"No, sir. Not at all. Just making a suggestion."

"So you think you're smarter than the coach, do you?"

Coach continued. "Listen; you'll do as I say around here! I don't want you thinking for yourself, or 'freestyling,' as you call it. Just for that smart-assed comment, you can sit on the bench the next game. Anybody else got any bright ideas they want to share?" No one said a word.

The next Friday night, we rode the bus to Rudyard for an away game. I didn't dress for the game and was forced to sit on the bench. By the end of the second quarter, we had scored only sixteen points to Rudyard's thirty. Coach herded us into the locker room at halftime and, as usual, slammed the door behind him. We knew we were in for a major ass-chewing. Coach paced back and forth in front of the lockers, not saying a word. The players sat silently, staring at their shoes, afraid to look up, waiting for the inevitable barrage. Finally, Coach grabbed a metal fold-up chair and hurled it across the room. It struck a full-length mirror, which shattered into a million pieces. Then he glared down at us, almost daring us to pick a fight with him.

"You guys call yourselves a basketball team? Are you shittin' me? We're getting our asses kicked out there; I'm not seeing much effort on that floor tonight. C'mon. Somebody step up and show a little leadership for once."

Coach walked over to Mo at the end of the bench. "Jenkins! You're being out-rebounded and out-played every time down the floor. You're a big guy, aren't you? Why can't you hold your ground?" Mo shrugged and looked away.

Then Coach looked at the rest of the team in wonder. "Why is it that our press breaks stink so badly tonight? We worked on that all week, but you'd never know."

Then he lined Larry up in his crosshairs. "And you, Madigan. You can't seem to stop anyone if your life depended on it. Your man's getting to the bucket every time."

Coach seemed like he was done trying to motivate the team. He had given up on us as a lost cause. All he wanted to do now was vent. His last words were: "You guys aren't fit to wear varsity uniforms. You're pitiful!" And he walked out.

After that speech, something seemed to die in that locker room. I knew the guys felt angry and disappointed in themselves, but I also knew they were fighters, every last one of them. Ever since grade school, we were used to winning. We hated to lose as much as the next team. The Mapleton Mavericks were, without a doubt, having a dismal season, and that didn't happen very often at this school. No one likes to be humiliated day after day, night after night. And certainly not by your own coach.

At the start of the season, the players had all bought into the coach's new system: the plays, the strategies, the defensive sets, but none of it was working as planned. We knew we were good basketball players overall, but so far this year, things were simply not going our way. We were told to execute the plays, not to create on our own. And for all our efforts, we were not only losing every game, but we were being slammed by our own coach. He was sucking the very spirit out of this team. So much for all that good sportsmanship stuff. At this point, I'd had enough.

Of course, no one would dare quit. That's what Coach expected some of us to do so he could blame the whole lousy season on lack of dedication and team effort. That would get him off the hook. But we wouldn't give him that satisfaction; we'd stick it out to the end, no matter what. We had hit rock bottom. Where else could we possibly go?

During lunch hour the next day, I decided to meet with Mo and Money to see how they felt. Some of the students were dissing the players in the hallways as losers and stopped coming to the home games. Game attendance had dwindled to mostly players' parents, friends, and of course, our loyal pep band. Local community fans had slipped away as well, not wanting to endure the agony of such a miserable season. They were used to better years at Mapleton.

Munching on his hamburger and fries, Mo broke the ice. "As far as I'm concerned, Coach Connors has gone too far; he's crossed the line, and I can't respect him anymore. He sure as hell doesn't respect the players."

Money nodded. "That guy doesn't deserve to coach a team at all. I can't stand the man."

"OK, guys," I said, "tell you what. It's time for a little payback. Let's make sure this jerk gets fired at the end of the season. We're 0-12 right now; let's go 0-22 for the year, and that should can his ass!"

Mapleton expected to field winning sports teams, so we doubted the athletic director would put up with a catastrophic season without making some changes. But if we were going to lose every game, we couldn't make it look obvious. We still had to put on a show of effort. Let the coach rage at halftime, pull his hair out, and scream his lungs out. We didn't care. It was our senior year, and we'd never have to play for him again. If we could get him fired for incompetence, we'd be sparing the players behind us years of agony and disgust. It was worth a try.

In school, we talked to a few of the other players, and they quickly agreed we had to find a way to get the coach dismissed. They promised to keep the plan quiet and not broadcast it to every player on the team. We held the cards, but only if we played them wisely.

Our next game was Senior Night with Gladstone coming to town. Before the game, each senior player was introduced along with his parents and paraded down the center of the gymnasium. The mothers received long-stemmed red roses, and the MC said a few words about each player, the total points he had scored in his high school career and the name of the college he planned to attend in the fall. The crowd was larger than usual, and for that special moment, we felt proud to play for the Mavericks. It was a welcome relief despite a losing season that couldn't end soon enough.

As the game progressed, the score see-sawed. Gladstone would go cold for a while, and we'd light it up. Then their defense would stiffen, and we'd commit one turnover after another. We clawed our way back in the fourth quarter, and with fifteen seconds to go in the game, we were down by only two points, with the ball in my hands as I drove down the court. It was a crazy, hectic moment with the crowd yelling and screaming for a victory. I glanced up at the people in the bleachers and saw my mother's face. She was shouting, "Put it in, Tommy! Put it in!"

My stomach churning, *the plan* flashed through my brain. Everyone in the gym was standing and hollering when I pulled up behind the three-point line and let it fly. With all eyes on that shot, it seemed to hang in the air for an eternity. Swish! All net! Holding a one-point lead and five seconds to go, the place went berserk. Mo and Money looked over at me as if to ask: What are you thinking?

On the inbounds play, Gladstone threw a bomb down the full length of the court, and we fouled them. They sank both free throws, and the air went completely out of the building. When I took that last shot, I wasn't thinking of the coach at all. I was only thinking of winning the game the way we used to. And for that brief moment, basketball was fun again. I wasn't executing any specific play called by the coach; I was playing for the sheer joy, the pure excitement of the game. I only wish it could have lasted.

We continued to work hard at scrimmages and practices, conditioning, and shooting drills. Coach screamed at us as usual, ranted and raved at everything he disliked, but something was very different about him. It was as if his soul had left the building; there was no longer any punch in his criticism. His heart wasn't in it anymore. The season had taken its toll on him. Still, we never heard a kind word from him all season long, not a single word of praise or encouragement. We felt his cold contempt, and perhaps he felt ours. Coach was probably too proud to consider we might be setting him up for the kill. In his mind, we were just a bunch of unskilled, thankless losers with no team pride. I could just imagine him thinking, *Wasn't my fault. I've done the best I could with what I had. They can't expect me to turn straw into gold. I'm a coach, not a magician.*

By early March, our season ended. We got whomped in the playoffs and, as predicted, wound up 0-22. It was a mixed blessing for us: On the one hand, it was a huge load off our shoulders, but on the other hand, we felt great disgust and humiliation and had to endure the brunt of endless jokes. We had brought it on ourselves, and now we had to own it.

You can probably guess what happened next. As expected, the athletic director fired Coach Connors. That is, his contract was not renewed for the following year. Everyone felt a great sense of relief. The last I heard, Coach moved back downstate; I'm not even sure if he's coaching anymore. But I really have no regrets.

Good sportsmanship is not all it's cracked up to be. Coaches from grade school on always taught us that winning wasn't everything—that it's all about competing hard on every play, and letting the chips fall where they may. At least, that's what they wanted us to believe. Treat everyone with respect, and they'll do the same for you–the golden rule of sports.

Except it doesn't always work out that way, especially when you're losing. Then, all the rules seem to fly out the window. Our coach didn't respect any of us as basketball players, so it was nearly impossible for us to play our hearts out for him. It was kind of an ugly and selfish thing for us to do as a team, but it felt like the only way to get any satisfaction from such a long, grueling season.

I wish the Mavericks well next year. The players are starving for victory. With a fresh start and a new coach, maybe it will be a winning season.

Letters from Maria

For as long as he could remember, Hank always had a plan. He believed problems were meant to be solved. If you approached one methodically, breaking it down into smaller pieces, the solution would present itself.

Beyond everything, Hank was optimistic, not in a blind or idiotic way, but with a cheerful, straightforward attitude. Years earlier, he had come across a copy of Dale Carnegie's *How to Win Friends and Influence People* and absorbed many of its principles. Some people thought Hank cocky and arrogant, but he would not let negative people get him down. He was sure-footed and upbeat, but realized there was no pleasing everybody.

Hank read material on a wide variety of subjects and researched problems to find the best solutions. Although he had his share of occasional bad luck, Hank believed he could always think his way through any difficulty without depending on good fortune to bail him out.

In 1981, after graduating from Northern Michigan University as a business major, he found himself the following summer working as a deckhand on the *Leon Fraser*, a 600-foot Great Lakes freighter that hauled iron ore cargoes between Duluth and Two Harbors down to the lower lakes in South Chicago and Conneaut, Ohio. Between college years in Marquette, Hank had obtained his Merchant Marine card from the Coast Guard and worked several summers on the boats to earn tuition money. He liked being independent and dreamed about someday owning a bookstore/coffee shop or becoming an investment broker. He could provide advice on buying and selling stocks and bonds. For now, Hank simply wanted to pay off the school loans that had piled up on him; he hated owing money to anyone.

Although Hank made good money on the ships, he missed his girlfriend, Maria, back in Marquette. She had just completed her junior year at NMU, majoring in French, and hoped to teach high school in a couple of years.

Maria loved Hank's energy and high spirits and how he wasn't afraid to tackle anything. He made her laugh with his off-color stories from the boats when he returned to school each fall. They had met in the theater during auditions for *My Fair Lady*. He heard her before he saw her; she had one of those high-pitched, contagious laughs you couldn't ignore. As they read lines from the script, she captivated him with her curly blond hair and mischievous blue eyes. Neither of them made callbacks, but within a week, he had asked her out for coffee.

Maria missed him terribly each summer when he left for the Soo to find a deckhand's job on the boats. She wanted him to find work in Marquette, but Hank insisted he could save twice as much on the ships. They exchanged letters every week he was away, and when summer ended, a heartfelt reunion seemed to renew their love completely.

To pay off his college loans and become debt-free as quickly as possible, Hank hatched an unusual plan. He would start by returning to the Great Lakes ships and saving everything he could. That way, he would retire his loans quickly, and save any accruing interest, instead of paying them down month after month for years. After giving it careful consideration, he had devised a workable plan for their future together.

"Why do you have to leave again to work on the boats?" Maria asked.

"Listen, I've got a proposal for us to consider. It'll get me out of debt quickly and set us up financially for the future."

Maria crossed her arms and turned her back to him. "You expect me to wait for you again all summer and longer? It's not that easy for me. I miss you."

"You have one more year in school," Hank explained, "and while you're studying, I can be earning good money. I've made a five-year plan where I will work on the freighters for five full seasons, save as much as possible—don't forget there's free room and board on the boats, no rent, no bills—and I'll invest my savings in stocks with a broker. If I've calculated things correctly, at the end of five years, I'll have enough for a good down payment on a house for us and enough left over to start a business. I've always wanted to work for myself. What do you say?"

Maria knew Hank was being sincere and methodical, maybe even wise, but it didn't seem workable to her. Was he at all concerned about the havoc this so-called plan might cause in their relationship? Had he bothered to factor that in? They had grown much closer in the past year, but being away on the boats had created its own set of stressful circumstances.

"I'm hoping," Hank continued, "that we can marry before too long and settle down somewhere."

"I want the same thing for us, but I'm going to need some time to think about this plan of yours."

Since Maria's senior year was coming up, she knew she'd be quite busy with her classes. She didn't mind Hank being away for a few weeks at a time, but when weeks turned into months, she became resentful and felt neglected. Now that Hank was proposing to work for a nine-month stretch on the Great Lakes for five straight seasons, she seemed reluctant and discouraged. He was asking an awful lot of her, even though he would be home every winter for three months. After some consideration, Maria told Hank she would give it a try, hoping he might change his mind.

By late May, Hank had secured a decking job aboard the *Arthur M. Anderson*, a U.S. Steel freighter hauling iron ore from the upper lakes to the lower ports. In a few weeks, he had settled in with the new crew and went confidently about his work. Some days, the deck crew scrubbed the white work and chipped paint; on other days, they hosed down iron-ore pellets that had spilled onto the deck during loading. In Duluth, the deckhands took their positions down on the dock, shifting the fore and aft cables to load the ship evenly. After a few hours, when loading was completed, they maneuvered the steel hatch covers back into place and tightened the many hundreds of hatch clamps to secure the cargo. There was never a shortage of work for the deck crew, and the days passed quickly.

When the work day was over, some crewmembers played cards or read newspapers. Hank had packed a suitcase full of novels and short stories and reveled in the free time he had to read them. This kind of freedom seldom materialized on shore. When he wasn't reading, he was usually writing Maria a letter. He told her about setting up an investment plan with a stockbroker back in Marquette, regularly sending in the bulk of his earnings to be invested in stocks and mutual funds. The market was very robust, so Hank's five-year plan was off to a good start.

Maria, meanwhile, had returned to school in the fall, but still found time to write letters to Hank on the boats. She waited tables at Vango's on the weekend and occasionally played folk guitar for a few hours at some of the local clubs. The tips she earned covered the cost of her textbooks and provided some pocket money.

By mid-January, Hank had made his last trip of the season, headed for winter layup in Sturgeon Bay, and returned to Marquette and Maria. Their reunions were electric, charged with an energy that had been stored up for many long months. Hank did not quite appreciate how neglected, how deprived, his senses had been during the long season on the lakes, but now everything came alive again when he held Maria in his arms—her perfume, her long silky hair, her soft skin, the warmth of her body—it was all so intoxicating. They melted into each other's arms and, for a moment, life had never been more satisfying. How, he wondered, could he ever have stayed away from her so long?

Their winter months together were a series of many late-night dinners with wine, candlelight, and long conversations. Weekend entertainment was often a potluck party at a friend's apartment; someone usually brought a guitar, and they sang songs late into the night.

One night during dinner, Maria felt it was a good time to talk about their future plans together. "Hank, have you reconsidered your plan at all? Maybe, I was thinking, you could find work here in town that you liked."

"I know how you're feeling, Maria, but we really should try to hang in there, if we can, for a few more years. My plan is working—since I have no bills to pay all season, my investments will pay off that much faster. You know I've thought this over quite seriously, and it's working just fine."

Maria frowned at him. "But what about us, Hank? Is it really working for us?"

"You have to be patient, Maria. This is just a short-term sacrifice for the long haul. Most young couples are buried in school debt when they graduate. I can't have that hanging over my head."

Maria got up from the table, walked across the living room, and curled up in an overstuffed chair. "So then, you feel your five-year plan is a short-term sacrifice on your part?"

Hank could feel himself being backed into a corner, so he tried to soothe her by gently kissing her forehead and hugging her. "Just trust me; think positive," he said. "Things will work out. They always do."

By early April, the ice was finally breaking up in the rivers, and another shipping season was underway on the Great Lakes. Hank had been shifted over to the *Cason J. Calloway* as a deckhand. After being cooped up all winter, he looked forward to the cool, sunny days on Lake Superior. In April, he still had to wear a down parka when on Lake Superior, but only a T-shirt on Lake Erie.

For Hank, leaving Maria in Marquette had been harder than usual, knowing she would be looking for work and probably moving somewhere before the end of summer. She had seemed edgy and uncertain all winter, and he wondered if he had made the right choice. His plan was solid, he reminded himself, and he did not want to waver. Hank was committed, but still felt uneasy.

One afternoon in early June, the *Calloway* was down bound at the Soo Locks. As it approached the MacArthur Lock, Hank hopped up on the bosun's chair and was swung out over the ship's side and lowered to the dock. The watchman threw him a heaving line, which he pulled until he had the heavier steel mooring cable in hand. The ship eased slowly into the first lock, and the deckhands slipped the cables over the bollards.

As the ship was lowered in the lock, Hank checked with the first mate to see if he wanted assistance picking up mail at the marine post office. Suddenly, he heard a familiar voice from the crowd of tourists behind the chain-link fence.

"Hey, sailor. You got a minute?"

Maria stood there, smiling and looking as pretty as ever. With her dark tan, white shorts, and pink halter-top, she took Hank's breath away.

"Wow! I didn't expect to see you here. You sure look amazing."

Hank rushed over to the fence and kissed her through the wires. He knew he had only a few precious minutes before he would have to climb back aboard the ship as it was lowered in the lock.

"I wanted to see you again before moving," she said, brushing her bangs from her eyes. "I found a job in Ann Arbor, teaching high school French, and I still have to find a place to live down there."

He wanted to leap over the fence and run away with her for the afternoon, but he tried to hold his feelings in check. "That's great! Congratulations! I miss you so much. I hope I can stay with you in Ann Arbor this winter. I'll call you when we get to port so we can make arrangements."

The mate had returned from the post office and was climbing back aboard ship, Hank's unspoken cue to follow him. Hank gave Maria one last kiss and scrambled back onboard. The brief reunion lasted only minutes, but Hank would replay it in his mind for weeks to come. Though he was very strong-willed, his resolve seemed to be weakening. He had great difficulty concentrating on his work, but he tried again to refocus on his goals.

Hank had always admired the chess grandmaster Bobby Fischer and the way he plotted his strategy half a dozen moves ahead of his opponent. He envisioned all the possible traps and failures, then went on the offensive, backing his opponent into a corner until it was too late. Hank tried to forge ahead with his own plan by preparing well, being proactive, and refusing to give up.

Along with the many novels he had brought onboard to read, Hank studied investment books by Wall Street gurus like Peter Lynch and Benjamin Graham. There was more to learn about finance and investment than he had ever dreamed, but he did not want to take unwarranted risks. Futures trading and commodity investing were much too complicated for him, even if the financial potential was tempting. Hank avoided individual stock picks and invested mostly in mutual funds and index funds. They were much safer because the risk was spread over a wide spectrum of individual companies within each fund family. His broker had also recommended several limited partnerships, although the commissions were a bit hefty. Little by little, Hank's nest egg was growing, just as he had planned so meticulously. He was proud of his progress so far.

Over the long summer months, Maria's letters came less frequently. She was quite busy moving, he realized, and probably did not have as much time to write. Sometimes he read her letters after dinner while sitting out on the hatch cover, the ship drifting lazily down the St. Mary's River. He could smell her perfume on the pages and wished he were home with her. In some of her letters, the words seemed distant, like her heart was not really in it, as though she were simply going through the motions. Maybe he had been on the boats for too long, he thought, and he was growing delusional or fearful. Was she losing interest in him? Had she met someone new?

Hank returned to his room below deck and tossed the latest letter in a drawer. To get his mind off things, he roped another deckhand into a few games of cribbage, nickel a point, down in the dunnage room.

By Christmas, the *Calloway* had hauled her last load of iron ore for the season, then headed for layup in Milwaukee. The ship's bow and many of the forward hatches were glazed with a heavy coat of stubborn ice, the result of relentless pounding waves that had frozen on contact. Many of the crewmembers had grown weary and short-tempered after working so many months out on the lakes. They were anxious to get back home to their families and friends.

On the final day of layup, Hank could not scramble off the ship fast enough. The long shipping season was over at last. With jubilant spirits and a racing heart, he rented a car and drove down to Ann Arbor to surprise Maria.

Although Maria was thrilled to see Hank again and hugged him warmly, she found her teaching job had become her top priority and absorbed most of her time. Between preparing daily lessons and grading homework, she barely had enough time to grocery shop and cook. For several winter evenings, they shared wine and more late-night talks, but Maria didn't seem as interested in his stories of life on the freighters. Her mind seemed to be elsewhere.

Maria noticed that Hank swore and used foul expressions more frequently; Hank was not aware of it until she pointed it out, but he apologized. He must have picked up some of the crew's jargon and crude manners without realizing it.

After spending a few days at Maria's apartment, Hank returned to Marquette for a short time to tie up some loose ends. He stayed with a close friend of his who had let Hank store his meager possessions while he was away on the lakes.

While in town, Hank planned to take a close survey of his investments and meet with his financial broker. After gathering all his necessary statements, he filed his income taxes and put that to bed for another year.

Many evenings, he hung out with some old friends. They reveled in his wild boat stories and marveled at his colorful adventures and tales of crazy characters he worked with. His friends asked if he was planning to make a career of being on the lakes, but Hank said he was simply saving enough to pay off his debts. He was reluctant to mention his five-year plan; that was between Maria and him. No point in bringing up a subject they could poke holes in, even jokingly. So far, he was still quite sure of himself, but subtle chinks were developing in his armor.

Hank soon returned to Ann Arbor to spend the winter with Maria. He moved a few small pieces of furniture and the rest of his miscellaneous possessions from Marquette down to Maria's apartment. Over the next few months, Hank helped out every way he could—by pitching in for rent and food, cooking most of the meals, and washing dishes and house cleaning whenever possible. Maria appreciated the effort and the time it freed up for her to devote to her lesson plans and preparations. They made time for long snowy walks in the woods and an occasional dinner at a favorite restaurant. Most importantly, they were able to spend time together—in conversation, laughing, drinking wine, and holding each other. They never felt happier.

With the new shipping season about to get underway, Hank headed for spring fit out, but found it near impossible to break away from Maria's loving arms. The winter months had flown by so swiftly. Hank was starting his third full year of sailing, this time as a deckhand on one of his old familiar boats, the *Leon Fraser*. He already knew several of the crewmembers and seemed to fit right in. For entertainment, he brought with him a cassette player and a shoebox of cassettes he had recorded over the winter from his extensive album collection—the Stones, the Eagles, Neil Young, as well as a mix of old blues artists.

As the summer wore on, the deck crew went about their usual jobs—rolling a fresh coat of red-lead paint on the deck, painting the hatch coamings, and scrubbing the white work fore and aft. The tourist traffic at the Soo Locks was peaking for the season as the *Fraser* locked through down bound. As the ship emerged from the lock, the supply ship *Ojibway* chugged out into the river to meet the *Fraser*, offloading pallets of paint, food, and equipment. When the crew had finished stowing all the supplies, Hank checked the mail and found a fresh letter from Maria. She hadn't been writing as often, but he attributed this slowdown to her hectic schedule. He was enjoying the warm summer evening as his ship cruised slowly down the St. Mary's River, past the shoreline cabins on Sugar Island and Neebish Island, and down through the rock cut at Barbeau.

Leaning against the railing, Hank opened her letter. It was only one page, not the usual three or four, and she got right to the point.

Dear Hank,

I'm very sorry to have to break this news to you in a letter but didn't think I had the nerve to say any of this to you in person. I don't think I can go on with this relationship any longer; I've tried my best to be patient but have grown tired waiting for you month after month. Things are simply not working out for us, regardless of The Plan. You are just too bull-headed and won't listen to any of my suggestions. Meanwhile, I have to be honest with you, I've started dating a few other friends, although I'll admit I still have strong feelings for you. I refuse to put my life on hold any longer, but I wish you the best. I'm sorry things turned out this way; I had no alternative.

All my best,

Maria

Hank reread the letter several times to make sure he wasn't missing something. He was stunned; his hands shook. Despite such a calm and peaceful evening on the river, his world was shattered. He crumpled the letter into a ball, flung it over the side, and watched it drift away in the current.

That evening, Hank crawled into his bunk early, without any dinner, but he couldn't sleep. His head was spinning with anger and confusion. A wave of helplessness swept through him, and questions haunted him all night long. *Had he been blind to all the signs Maria was showing? He'd known her patience was dwindling, but why had she totally abandoned his plan? Had he been so stubborn that he couldn't see the obvious? Had she been seeing someone else all along? Did Maria not love him anymore?* The questions hounded him relentlessly until, exhausted, he drifted into a fitful sleep.

For the next few days, Hank did not do well at all. He wrestled with his options and focused on every possible way to alter his plans. Black coffee was the only thing that interested him. His appetite had disappeared. The other crewmembers noticed Hank's faraway demeanor and tried to shake him out of his funk, but he was helplessly distant.

One morning, Hank absentmindedly kicked over a bucket of paint, tripped over the raised deck plating, and nearly toppled into the cargo hold through an open hatch. The bosun took one long look at him and yelled, "Snap out of it, you sonofabitch, before you kill yourself!"

When the ship tied up in port to unload cargo for a few hours, Hank went up the street to the nearest bar and phoned Maria. He pleaded with her to come back to him, insisting he loved her dearly and that she just needed to have a little more patience. He mentioned that his investments for their future were doing well and that his plan, as frustrating as it was for her, would pay off in the long run.

"Don't you understand?" she said. "I can't live this way. I feel so abandoned. I don't want to see you anymore."

"Maria, we can work this out somehow, if we just take the time to think our way through this."

"That's just it. You always want to think it through, but there's no feeling. You're all head and no heart. I'm done with this. I hate your plan."

She hung up on him. Hank dropped the receiver and ordered a whiskey at the bar. His world had gone haywire, but he was grimly determined to stick with his plan as long as possible, despite his personal setback. *There must be a solution to this problem,* he thought. *Maybe Maria will have a change of heart. Give her some time.*

One day, several weeks later, as the *Leon Fraser* made her way down the Detroit River, the mail boat pulled alongside the ship. The mate lowered a five-gallon bucket to pick up mail and newspapers, and Hank bought a *Detroit Free Press* to catch up on some of the news. After dinner, quickly scanning the newspaper, he noticed the bold headlines: "Dow Average Loses 800 Points in One Day." He wondered about his investments, but he wasn't able to get to a phone while out on the lakes.

A few days later, Hank finally reached his stockbroker in Marquette. Due to troubles in the Middle East and investor anxiety, his investments had lost nearly 40 percent of their value; thousands of dollars in savings had vanished overnight. Wall Street was in a tailspin, and the market was circling the drain. In Hank's mind, losing money so drastically was never part of the plan. Saving prudently for a life with Maria was a mental discipline he knew he could handle, but he had not realistically allowed for any major setbacks in the financial markets. That was totally out of his control.

Hank thought he might have to work a couple of extra years on the boats to make up for his losses. But what was the point now? Maria had left him and was not coming back. What use was a five-year plan without her?

After dinner that evening, Hank walked up and down the deck, trying to burn off his mounting anxiety. The other deck-hands tried to interest him in a poker game, but Hank couldn't focus on cards. He needed to find a wild card solution before throwing in his hand.

In the past, Hank had always been able to find an answer to any problem that presented itself. His method was simply to gather the facts and as much relevant information as possible and search for practical solutions. Some problems were more difficult than others, but in the end, there was always a logical answer. He believed in it; he swore by it—be calm and rational and things will always work out.

But this time, he was stymied. He had run into a wall that felt insurmountable. His natural tendency was to double down and work that much harder, but for once, he was unable to find his always-reliable inner resolve. It had abandoned him without warning. Hank tried to focus on his daily work—chipping, painting, hosing down the deck—but his mind wandered. His heart wasn't in it anymore.

When Hank crawled into his bunk that night, he played a mix-tape of the Eagles and the Stones on his tape player. The ship was steaming down Lake Michigan on its way to Chicago. Through the open porthole, he could see the full moon. Hank had turned down the lights in his room and plugged in his Walkman headphones so he could drift off to sleep listening to the music. A couple of songs he kept rewinding and playing over again. The Eagles' "Desperado" was stuck in his mind: The words, about letting somebody love you and not waiting until it's too late, struck a nerve. The plaintive piano chords echoed in his memory and haunted his thoughts. Then the Stones came on with "You Can't Always Get What You Want," lamenting our blindness when it comes to understanding our real needs. Hank slowly realized he was letting someone he dearly loved slip away, that he'd been crippled by his own single-mindedness and regimented self-discipline. His commitment to logic and rational thinking had nearly destroyed the one thing that meant so much to him—Maria's love. *Perhaps there is a way to compromise,* he thought, *and not be so pig-headed about everything?* Time was now of the essence.

Hank drifted off to sleep peacefully that night, feeling as though a crushing weight had been lifted off his chest. He felt himself letting go, abandoning the control he once felt so necessary. His orderly, disciplined world was suspended for now, and for the first time in a long while, Hank slept deeply until morning.

~ ~ ~

On a warm August evening, Maria heard a soft knock at her door. She was just about to pull some baked whitefish from the oven before settling down to work on lesson plans for fall classes. When she opened the door, Hank was smiling at her with a sea bag over his shoulder.

"Hey, good lookin', something smells good."

"Hank! Oh, my God!"

Maria hugged him but quickly pulled away, unsure what to make of this surprise. "What are you doing here? I thought you were still sailing on the freighters."

"Not anymore. I quit. For good. I couldn't live . . . without you in my life."

"What about your plan?" asked Maria.

Hank shrugged. "We can always make a new plan together. I've missed you too much just to let you go. If you could just give me another chance, I would—"

Maria threw her arms around Hank and kissed him tenderly. She would not let him go. In that lingering moment, the only thing that mattered was the two of them, lost in each other's warm embrace. Together now, they would let their lives unfold one day at a time, with or without a plan.

Crisp Point

It was Mandi's idea originally, to drive up to the U.P. for spring break. All our friends were headed south to the usual places like Fort Lauderdale and Cancun to party and lay in the sun. We'd already played that card during other school breaks and wanted to experience something different, something totally off-the-wall and spontaneous. This was our senior year of college—the proud class of 2019—and probably our last chance to have some fun before getting serious about our careers.

Upper Michigan would be a great destination in early March, too early for the flood of summer tourists and pesky mosquitoes, and not an unreasonably long drive from our campus in Milwaukee. Neither one of us had ever been to the U.P. before, and we thought it would be exciting to explore some of the wilder and more remote places up north.

Mandi and I have shared an off-campus apartment our last couple of years at school. In fact, we've shared a lot of things like clothes, makeup, and on occasion, even boyfriends. But I'm getting off the track. What I really want to tell you about is this bizarre road trip that literally went off the tracks.

The morning after I finished my last mid-term exam in macro-economics, Mandi and I quickly packed a few things in my old Honda Civic and struck out for the U.P. I called my mom and told her we were driving up north to Tahquamenon

Falls for a few days and that I would call her when we got there. She worries a lot when I travel and always feels better if I check in. I'd probably be the same if I ever had a young daughter. But Mandi and I are very capable women; we just haven't had much wilderness experience.

By the time we had picked up some food supplies, it was early afternoon. We had driven as far north as Manistique on northern Lake Michigan when twilight fell. We found a cheap hotel on the water with off-season rates and crashed for the night, hoping to get a fresh start in the morning.

The farther north we drove, the colder it got, even though spring wouldn't officially arrive for a couple more weeks. A few inches of snow still lingered on the ground, with temperatures hovering in the middle thirties. Hardly a soul was walking or driving around town the night we pulled in. We had an eerie feeling we were passing through a ghost town. High overhead, the stars sparkled on this dark, moonless night. We could viscerally sense the U.P.'s remoteness and stark isolation, an undisturbed wintry wilderness. I didn't quite feel comfortable and prayed I wouldn't hear a pack of hungry coyotes howling in the woods. Nighttime often stirs my imagination too vividly; I sometimes see shadows and hear noises that just aren't there. We could hardly wait for daylight to chase it all away.

After breakfast, we drove up 77 to M-28, then north on 123 just past Newberry. By noon, we had arrived at the upper falls of Tahquamenon State Park. Apparently, we had beat the crowds by several months since there were only two other cars in the massive parking lot. We had the whole place to ourselves.

Five or six inches of snow lingered on the ground as we hiked through the woods and down the hundred or so steps to the platform overlooking the upper falls. The river was the color of rusty iron ore and quite spectacular in its dramatic plunge to the churning waters below. Mandi and I had seen a video on YouTube earlier of a Brazilian guy going over the fifty-foot falls in a kayak. It was insane, but he survived. He was a professional who had planned this stunt for many months and apparently filmed it. Partly because of that crazy kayaker, Mandi and I had decided to come here for spring break. Maybe it was the draw of the area's secluded beauty and perhaps the need to experience unfamiliar territory. But you couldn't pay me enough to do what that kayaker did; the guy has major cojones.

During a mid-afternoon lunch at the Brewery, which was right in the middle of the park, Mandi came across a brochure for Crisp Point Lighthouse. The two-track trail was just up the road from the falls and meandered through the woods to the lighthouse on Lake Superior.

"Jennifer," Mandi said, "Crisp Point on this map is no more than fifteen miles from here. We've got at least a couple of hours of daylight left. What do you say?"

I studied our Michigan roadmap, which didn't offer much detail about remote trails.

"Well, the road doesn't look paved," I noted, "but if we can get in and out before dark, I'm game. Might be fun . . . and a little adventurous."

I tried calling my mom to let her know we had made it to the falls, but I had only one bar on my cell and couldn't reach her. Just down the road from the park entrance, we found the trail to the lighthouse. As expected, it was a two-track with no signs of recent travelers.

The Honda snaked slowly through the woods, following the primitive trail northward. It dipped and rose through massive puddles from the spring melt, surrounded by scrubby jack pines and bare-limbed birches. At one point, the narrow road diverged into two paths, with no signage pointing the way to Crisp Point. We took the one to the right since it looked more heavily worn.

After an hour's worth of slow, careful driving down this impossible trail, we came to a sharp incline and stopped in the middle of a large, muddy puddle. The Honda didn't have much ground clearance, and I didn't want to scrape off my exhaust system. As I slowly accelerated, the tires began to spin, digging deeper into the black muck. I threw it in reverse and tried to rock it–forward, reverse, forward, reverse–but the car wouldn't budge.

Mandi stumbled out of the car, and I followed. The front wheels were buried in eight inches of murky water, and it looked like the low-slung car frame was getting hung up. We stared helplessly at the stalled vehicle, trying not to panic.

"Okay, okay," Mandi cautioned, pacing around the car. "We've got to keep our cool. We can figure this out if we just think clearly." Within two hours, the woods could be black as coal. This was no place to be stranded.

"Omigod, we are so screwed. We shouldn't have taken a chance on this shitty little trail."

"Calm down, Jennifer! We'll be all right. Let's get some branches or wood under those front tires."

We broke off branches from a few pine trees and gathered some downed smaller pieces in the clearing. Then we jammed them under the tires. Mandi jumped back in the car and shifted it into drive. The branches shot out from under the wheels as she floored the gas pedal. The car dug down deeper into the muck and refused to budge.

We guessed we were maybe ten miles from the main road, no more than four or five from the lighthouse. Our tennis shoes were soaked, and we were both splattered with mud and debris. Finally, we decided to call a wrecker, if we could even find one out in this wilderness. But I had forgotten to charge my phone that morning, so it was completely dead. We kept reminding ourselves, *We are grown women; we can handle this.* We both began to cry but quickly stopped. We had to think clearly; this was no time to panic.

We estimated that walking back to the main road would be about a three-to-four-hour trek, if we could even follow the trail back through the darkening woods. By this time, we had only an hour's worth of daylight; fortunately, we had remembered to bring a small LED flashlight.

Our best bet, we decided, would be to spend the night in the car and walk out in the morning. Nothing was to be gained by getting lost in the dark and freezing to death. So we scrambled back into the car, pulled out whatever sweaters and sweatshirts were available, and added every layer we could–two pairs of socks and mittens, but no hats. We would have to stay warm all night and wisely ration the gas.

Since we hadn't really planned to camp, we had food-shopped accordingly. Our stash consisted of two bottles of cabernet, water, a loaf of crusty French bread, sliced salami, a small brick of Swiss cheese, and a jumbo-size bag of Doritos. As darkness fell, Mandi and I sat in the front seat pretending to have a spring picnic, trying to keep our minds off wolves, bobcats, or other wild animals that might be lurking in the nearby woods. After all, we were safe in the car; nothing could harm us.

Every twenty minutes or so, we turned the ignition on to warm the car, but only for a few minutes. The windows were cracked slightly so we wouldn't asphyxiate ourselves. During these brief spurts, we plugged in the phone charger, hoping to juice up the phone enough to call out. The wind started to rise in the trees, but cloud cover obscured the night sky. Sipping her wine, Mandi and I looked out into the blackness of the woods and tried to keep our minds on things we could handle. Maybe we had both seen too many Halloween thriller movies and didn't want to entertain any wild thoughts about a friendly visit from Freddie Krueger.

Abruptly changing the subject, Mandi said, "So, Jennifer, with graduation right around the corner, have you heard anything since you applied to Google and Microsoft?"

"No, nothing so far, but I'm expecting an answer soon. San Francisco or Seattle would be a welcome change for me; I've never lived out west."

"Yeah, but won't you miss the Great Lakes and all the kayaking and swimming right in our backyard?"

"Well, don't forget, California has plenty of beaches. Maybe I'll become a surfer babe with a bronzed body, and all the cute guys will be drooling over me."

Mandi laughed and poured herself some more wine. "As for me, I'd like to move out to New York and find a job in fashion merchandising, so I'm going to hold off getting married until I'm maybe thirty-five or forty. Even if I find the right guy, he's gonna have to wait for me. There's no rush to marry and have kids early. In fact, I plan to freeze my eggs and thaw them out when I'm good and ready."

Suddenly, we heard a loud rustling in the underbrush, like an animal plowing its way through. Then a low growl–the voice of a predator or prowler.

"What the hell was that?" Mandi whispered, looking in

the sound's direction.

I couldn't see anything yet, but the steady crunching sound of something moving across the dark, snowy field was getting louder. "I'll shine the flashlight," I said.

"No, you idiot; it will know we're here," Mandi whispered.

It was nearly nine o'clock by now, and our eyes were starting to adjust to the dark. A large black shadow lumbered toward the car, raising its head occasionally to sniff the air. As it came within ten feet of the car, we could see it was unmistakably a full-grown black bear. Mandi held her index finger up to her lips to make sure I stayed quiet. But the bear must have heard us or smelled us due to the windows being slightly rolled down. With a loud growl, it suddenly lunged at the car in the dark, maybe assuming it was another predator. We both screamed, thinking he was about to rip off the car doors.

"Do something, Mandi!" I cried.

While she started the car and began honking the horn relentlessly, I grabbed my LED flashlight and shined it in the bear's face. We didn't know if the bear was male or female, but we knew it must be hungry—it had probably just woken from hibernation. Jennifer and I rolled up the windows so the animal couldn't get a good grip on the doors.

"He smells the salami and cheese in here!" I shouted. "Should we just throw the food out there to get rid of him?"

"No! No! That would just encourage him."

The bear rambled round and round the car, looking for an entry point. Meanwhile, Mandi honked the horn repeatedly, which the bear completely ignored. After about twenty minutes, the animal seemed to lose interest and staggered off into the woods. We had to pee badly but waited another half-hour, to be safe, before opening the car door.

We stayed awake the entire night, too nervous to sleep. Listening for suspicious noises in the woods, we prayed the bear would not return. Every half hour or so, when we began to shiver from the cold, Mandi started the car up and ran the heater for a few minutes, trying to conserve our gas supply as long as possible. Finally, my cellphone had charged up enough to try to call out, but again, we must have been in a dead zone. No response.

When daylight arrived, we tried calmly to assess our situation. It was a cold, gray morning with the wind swirling in the treetops, dropping random clumps of snow from the upper branches. Our food and water were almost completely used up, so we knew we would have to abandon the car's safety. The gas tank was nearly empty, so another night in the car would likely bring on hypothermia. It was either backtrack down the trail to the main road or hike to the lighthouse at Crisp Point, which we judged was less than a two-hour hike. Our core body temperatures had dropped significantly, so a vigorous hike would help warm us.

"There's no way," I said, "that we can walk down that trail to the main road. That's the direction the bear headed last night."

"Yeah, you're right," Mandi agreed, "but he could be anywhere by now."

"It's a much shorter walk to the lighthouse. Maybe we can find somebody there to help us, or we can try to make another call out."

"Do you think anyone's looking for us now?" Mandi asked.

"I really doubt it," I said. "My mom knows we were headed for the falls, but beyond that, she has no idea we're up here in the woods."

It was late morning when we set out for the point. Dead grass showed through a thin layer of snow on the trail, and a light covering of ice skimmed the melting puddles. We had filled a small daypack with our remaining food and grabbed the cellphone that was now partially charged up. The next few miles were not as treacherous as the ones we'd driven through, and we knew the beach was getting closer. The two of us walked briskly through the woods, looking back occasionally to see if we were being followed.

When we finally sighted the lighthouse in the distance, Mandi and I began galloping joyously, racing toward a hopeful sign of assistance. But the entire place was abandoned, not a soul in sight. No lightkeeper, no houses in the area, and obviously, no park rangers. Our hearts sank. We were getting in deeper, and our luck seemed to be running out.

The only visible shelter out of the wind appeared to be the Crisp Point Lighthouse, a tall white circular structure made of bricks. As Mandi and I scanned the nearby area, my eye caught some movement back near the edge of the woods from where we had just walked. A black shadowy form emerged in the clearing, about a hundred yards away.

"Oh, shit!" Mandi yelled. "That damn bear has been tracking us. C'mon!"

We raced toward the lighthouse, praying it was unlocked. It was not. We looked back, and the bear was getting closer. Mandi stood back and kicked hard at the door with the heel of her hiking boots. That loosened it a bit, so I slammed my shoulder into the door as hard as possible. It swung open with a stubborn squeal. We tried to lock it behind us, but the lock was now busted. We scrambled up the narrow spiral staircase until we reached the top. From the height of the tower, we could see the bear only twenty yards away now, sniffing the air to pick up our scent. He stumbled toward the lighthouse; then we lost sight of him. Suddenly, we heard him butting his head against the door below us and growling angrily. We were trapped in the tower and worried that this cunning black brute would try climbing the narrow stairs. Apparently nothing could stop him. We had always heard that bears were never aggressive with humans unless a food source was nearby. And this one had seemingly just come out of hibernation and was following his nose.

Mandi glanced at me with tears in her eyes, trying to maintain her cool. She was always the stronger one whenever trouble showed up. I couldn't help but cry and felt a stream of warm pee trickling down my thigh.

"Let's call someone," Mandi pleaded.

I whipped out my cellphone and, from the height of the lighthouse, I now had several bars. I pressed 9-1-1 and someone quickly answered.

"This is 9-1-1. What is your emergency?"

"Oh! Thank God! This is Jennifer and Mandi, and we are trapped in the Crisp Point Lighthouse. A bear is trying to attack us at the bottom of the stairway. Can you please help us immediately? Please!"

The dispatcher quickly swung into action, calling the authorities near Paradise, just a few miles south of Whitefish Point.

Meanwhile, the angry growl of the bear echoed in the stairwell. To stall matters, Mandi and I dug frantically through our daypack and pulled out the remaining cheese, salami, bread, and Doritos, broke them into small pieces, and flung them to the bottom of the stairway. The bear was briefly distracted and sniffed the offering inquisitively before gobbling the suspicious tidbits. We tried stretching what little food we had for as long as possible and even poured the remaining wine down the stairwell. Every time the bear growled, we threw a few more morsels to pacify his hunger.

After what seemed like an eternity, probably about thirty minutes, help was on the way. Off in the distance, toward the shoreline, we heard the dull hum of high-speed engines. We looked toward the beach and saw two yellow snowmobiles approaching us. We screamed, and Mandi took off her red nylon windbreaker and waved it at them wildly. They didn't see us at first, but they did notice the bear trying to get through the lighthouse door. As the snowmobilers approached, the roar of the machines apparently spooked the bear, and he turned and trotted away toward the woods.

Mandi and I quickly stumbled down the spiral steps, crying uncontrollably, and hugged both drivers. We clung to them tightly for the longest time. As emergency volunteers, they had been dispatched from Paradise. The fastest way to get to us, they figured, was to snowmobile straight down the shoreline from Whitefish Point. They had arrived in the nick of time, as we had exhausted our food supply. The sled drivers, Joe and Billy, hadn't expected anyone at the lighthouse this time of the year. In fact, they said, the bear might have been a little disoriented too. He had probably just come out of hibernation, maybe a week or two early, and was ravenous for food. Despite our wet shoes and cold feet, our thirst and hunger pangs, we had not a single thing worth complaining about. We felt exhausted from the prolonged rush of adrenaline.

Joe and Billy drove us back to Paradise on their snowmobiles to help find a wrecker. We got the Honda pulled out later that afternoon and steered for home. The prospect of returning to school to frantically finish our last semester–more books to study, papers to write, and final exams—seemed almost warm and inviting by comparison to our night in the woods. It's wise to be prepared for surprises, but next time we might not be so lucky. The unexpected can happen to anyone, even two fairly resourceful women. We were being chased, this time, only by deadlines.

3

REGRETS

Whiteout

In Michigan's Upper Peninsula, there are winter snow-storms that wreak havoc on land, but these same blizzards can often disorient and blind any fisherman brave enough to venture out on an open expanse of frozen water. Normally, I'd consider myself to be a fairly cautious, well-prepared sort of person. I'm not usually one to let my guard down, but this particular episode caught me totally by surprise.

About three years ago, my friend Allen and I both retired from working for Chippewa County. I had worked in the Treasurer's office, and he was in the Register of Deeds. We both liked to hunt and fish, especially in the winter. Al had built his own shack to ice-fish on the upper St. Mary's River. By early February every year, he hauled it out on the ice and set it in about six feet of water so he could spear- or line-fish. Usually, he caught his limit of whitefish or perch and often shared them with me.

The two of us had been good buddies since we had fought together in Vietnam, where we each served our year of duty back in the '60s. Allen was always stubborn and independent-minded back then, hard to persuade once he'd made up his mind. So, after the Army, he went one way, and I went the other, but we both returned to the Soo and wound up working together years later. Just luck, I guess.

Allen never married or had a family; it just wasn't particularly important to him. He liked his freedom too much and never wanted to feel tied down. He stayed in good shape, too, much better than me. I've put on probably forty pounds more than I should—too many cheeseburgers and beer. But Allen got his exercise walking and biking wherever he went. No need for him to belong to a gym; he took good care of himself. That's why I don't understand how he got himself in such a bind. He was always so methodical and self-disciplined, so well-prepared in everything he did.

It was a frosty Saturday morning in early March when Al headed out to his fish shack on the upper river. The ice had been melting and freezing for several days, so sometimes you could see open water way out in the river. In a few weeks, everyone would have to remove their shacks from the bay to make way for the shipping season. The ore freighters, the size of several football fields, would be opening the season in late March after the Coast Guard icebreakers had busted up the frozen channel.

Allen usually hauled his equipment on a toboggan—his wood for the stove, his lunch, bait—and hiked the hundred yards or so from shore for the exercise. Most of the other fishermen rode their snowmobiles out to their shacks, but Al thought they were just lazy, spoiled by high technology and too much retirement money. They probably all had electric snow blowers and riding lawn mowers, he often said, and would never get a decent day's worth of exercise.

But Al was wise enough to carry a simple cellphone to call friends, if the fish weren't biting, or for an emergency. This particular morning, he had asked me to come out and fish with him, but I was busy with a few other household jobs and couldn't make it.

When Al called me about mid-afternoon, he seemed to be

in good spirits. He'd caught several whitefish by jigging wax worms. The fish were attracted by the canned corn he spread on the sandy bottom for feed. He planned to fish until early evening, about six o'clock. A lot of fishermen believe the fish bite better in early twilight. Meanwhile, he said he had finished his lunch of ham-and-cheese sandwiches, washed down with a couple of shots of Jack Daniels. Al usually brought his *Detroit Free Press* to read during slow times, to catch up on the Red Wings and the Pistons and all the hoopla back in Washington, D.C.

Al didn't mind being all by himself out there on the ice. He never felt lonely or bored and said it was a relaxing way to spend his retirement. From a health standpoint, I worried about him a little if there were an emergency, but he was always in good health.

About 7 p.m., my phone rang, and Al was not quite himself. He tried to sound calm, but I could hear the alarm and fear in his voice. An unexpected winter storm had moved into the area.

"Ray, this is Al. Can you hear me?" he shouted. I could hear the wind howling in the phone and Al's labored breathing.

"Yes, Al, I hear you. Are you on your way back to shore?"

"I don't know for sure," Al said, nearly out of breath. "I left my shack twenty minutes ago, and I'm a little turned around. This squall came in out of nowhere, and I can't see a damned thing."

Apparently, the temporary squall he had expected had turned into a full-blown winter blizzard with high winds and falling temperatures. The lights on shore, which he normally used as a guide, were no longer visible.

"Have you checked your compass yet?" I asked.

"I left it in my other jacket pocket when I changed this morning."

The wind kept howling in my ear, and I had a hard time hearing him.

"I should've stayed in my shack until the storm blew over!" Al shouted. "But I ran out of wood and started getting cold. Can't seem to find my way back now . . . . My tracks disappeared."

"Hang in there, Al. I'm calling for help right now."

"Don't bother, Ray; I'll find my way out of this and get back to you in—" Then his phone suddenly cut out.

I knew Al was scared out of his wits but trying to remain calm. This situation could not be easy for someone normally so well-prepared. I called the Coast Guard and the sheriff's department. They agreed to dispatch a search-and-rescue team immediately.

Usually, the hike from Al's shack to the mainland is no more than fifteen or twenty minutes, even if you're pulling a toboggan full of gear. In the dark, with the snow blowing sideways, Al had been walking long enough to make shore but must have gotten off course.

After so much time, hypothermia and disorientation could set in, and there was no place to take shelter out there. Al was at the mercy of the elements, and these spring storms can be vicious on Lake Superior.

I pulled on my boots, threw on my winter parka, and raced in the truck to meet the sheriff's people. I drove a few miles west of the Soo to the upper river where Al's car was parked. The storm was blowing so hard I could barely see the road. I thought of Al wandering around on the ice, half-frozen and delirious, and felt sick. As long as I've known Al, he has never been the kind of guy to take chances out on the ice; it was always safety first with him. I know he was cold, but he should've stayed put in his shack, out of the wind. I should've been there with him.

A couple of winters ago, Al lost a good friend over on Lake George, to the east of Sugar Island. It was in the springtime, late March, when this guy had driven his pickup out on the ice to fish and had fallen through and drowned. He got trapped under the ice in his vehicle. Al would never have taken that sort of chance, but people still do it.

I remember hearing about a few snowmobilers a couple of years ago who were riding out on the ice late one night, following the Canadian shoreline about a hundred yards out. They were bar-hopping that night, and on their way back home, for a little excitement, they decided to jump some ice floes over open water. To me, that's practically suicide. One of them jumped just short of the next ice floe and crashed into the icy water and drowned. They say a person has less than two minutes to crawl out of ice water before his muscles become limp and useless. I doubt Al would have ever done such a reckless thing.

I tried calling Al's cellphone over and over again, but he wouldn't answer. Battery must have died. *The poor fellow's probably frozen stiff by now*, I thought. By the time the sheriff's people arrived, the storm was letting up somewhat. The rescue team fanned out near the shore and shone their powerful flashlights out into the darkness on the river. They called out for Al, but there was no answer. As the wind diminished, the searchers made their way out to his shack, but no one was there.

As we called out for Al and searched the area with our lights, I vaguely recalled an old Jack London story, "To Build a Fire." A man freezing in the Alaskan wilderness had finally kindled a small fire under a fir tree, only to have a clump of melting snow from a branch above fall on the fire and douse it. The helpless man could do no more physically as hypothermia set in. It was a gradual, almost peaceful, feeling as his body shut down and drowsiness slowly overcame him. I feared for Al's life at that moment, but I still held out hope.

After searching for hours, including with the aid of a Coast Guard helicopter, the sheriff's people finally had to quit for the night. At that point, the search-and-rescue had, by necessity, turned into a body recovery. We would have to wait until morning to continue.

By daylight, the searchers had returned to comb the area thoroughly. They dispatched divers into the icy waters of the upper river, and within a few hours, discovered the body under the ice. Poor Al must have gotten totally turned around and thought he was walking toward shore, only to walk right out to the open river. They found his toboggan near the edge of the ice field.

It's a damned shame. My good friend Al should never have suffered such a horrible death. It was preventable, in my opinion, if only he hadn't panicked and taken matters into his own hands. If hypothermia can lull you into a sleepy delirium, I hope Al went peacefully. The guy loved ice-fishing and died doing what he loved most. I miss him dearly. To this day, I no longer let any friend of mine ice-fish by himself. I feel responsible for Al; in many ways, it was my fault, and I had to learn the hard way. We have to take care of the ones we love. When they're gone, they're gone.

When the Rooster Crows

Frank Parcello was not the type to be bullied easily. Though he was only 5' 9" and 175 pounds, he always stood his ground. His BS detector was better than most, and he could smell a rat a mile away.

Living in the Upper Peninsula, near Brimley, suited Frank just fine–no traffic like downstate, no crowds, and quiet enough to hear himself think. Some people didn't care for the isolation and hard winters, but as far as Frank was concerned, they could quit their bitching and move back to the city tomorrow. Good riddance. No sweat off his back. The U.P. suited him just fine.

For nearly a year, Frank had retired from his tire-and-battery business, known locally as Frank's Tire Shop. He had run a steady business for more than thirty-five years, a solid and predictable cash cow that had earned him and his wife a good living, especially for a small town so far up north. People needed good tires and batteries year round, and he liked the simplicity of such a reliable business model. He had advertised frequently on the radio and in local papers to undercut his competitors by a few bucks whenever possible.

Monday through Saturday, Frank had worked in his shop, always busy with his many loyal customers who liked the way he treated them. "If you expect to get through the winter, you gotta have good tires and a good battery," Frank often said.

"And if you want good traction in the winter, you need snow tires, not those wimpy all-season radials." As Frank would say, "You need good rubber if you expect to live up here." He was always full of safe-driving pointers and one-liners: "Don't try to squeeze the last few miles out of those old bald tires unless you feel lucky. You'll be in the ditch before you know it." The customers usually listened to him and followed his advice.

Many years earlier, Frank had managed a retail sports store in Traverse City, but he had yearned to strike out on his own. With a bachelor's in business from MSU, he intended to work for himself one day and call his own shots. When Frank and Emily got married, he had talked her into moving back up north and buying a farmhouse with ten acres west of Brimley. It would be a fresh start for them.

Jobs were hard to come by when Frank and Emily arrived in '82, but Emily had found part-time work as a waitress at a local bar-restaurant that specialized in serving whitefish dinners. While Frank renovated the old farmhouse, she earned enough to pay the bills. They endured their share of life's bumps and bruises. After an early miscarriage, Emily could no longer have children, but they had slowly adjusted to that. Before long, they purchased an abandoned gas station at a busy intersection and started their new tire business. It took several years to smooth out all the obstacles, but eventually it all came together. The two of them were happy with their ambitious efforts and their busy life together.

Then, at sixty-two, Emily unexpectedly died. It happened two months after Frank had sold the tire shop, retired, and was planning to travel extensively with his wife. Emily had always seemed quite healthy, didn't smoke, and only drank a glass of red wine now and then, but a heart attack suddenly struck her.

Frank was shattered. He had depended on Emily for so much–companionship, meals together, conversation, someone to hold in bed on a cold night. Now that was all gone, taken away from him without warning, and he wasn't sure what he would do next. Frank was retired and alone in his farmhouse with ten acres. Their dream of retiring and traveling around the country in a motor home had abruptly vanished. The thought of traveling everywhere by himself did not appeal to Frank at all.

After forty years of marriage, Frank was not having an easy time adapting to his new single life. Most evenings, he was pounding down a six-pack of beer, followed by several shots of Evan Williams. He usually fell asleep in front of the TV watching sports or old movies. For dinner, he often picked up frozen pizza or fast-food burgers. His wife had usually cooked dinners for them–meatloaf, chicken dishes, spaghetti–but Frank had little desire to grocery shop or put together full meals. *Why bother,* he thought, *when there's just me?*

After six months of mourning and brooding, Frank knew he needed some kind of female companionship. The farmhouse was much too quiet and isolated. No one to talk with, to listen to his opinions, or laugh at his lame jokes. He was sick of yelling at the political pundits on TV. They thought they had everything figured out, but he gave them an earful with his running commentary. Still it was not the same as having another person in the room to talk to.

One weekend, Frank decided to comb the bars in town—to shake the bushes, as he called it. He wasn't used to bar-hopping anymore, but that's where the women seemed to be. As Willie Sutton replied when asked why he robbed banks, "Because that's where the money is." Right away, Frank noticed most of the bar clientele were in their twenties and thirties, much too young for his taste. By the time he stopped at the Sunset

Lounge, he was about to call it a night when he ran across a pretty redhead nursing a cocktail at the bar. Somewhere in her late forties, he guessed, Leah was smoking a Marlboro and sipping a gin-and-tonic. Pulling up a barstool next to her, Frank ordered a beer and nervously tossed an opener: "Kind of a quiet place here tonight . . . . When does all the fun begin?"

Leah smiled at him and introduced herself. "This is about as good as it gets at this place. At least the drinks are reasonable." She tapped her ashes into the tray.

"This is the first bar I've been to in probably ten years," he confessed.

"Really?" she said. "Were you on the wagon, or is drinking against your religion?"

"No, I just haven't had any good reason to come to a bar. But my wife died six months ago, and I needed to come out and see the bright lights and big city."

"Sorry to hear that," she said. "Sounds like you needed a change of pace, something to get your mind off things."

"Yeah, something like that, I guess." Frank couldn't quite figure her out. Leah seemed warm and caring one minute, then distant and detached the next. *Maybe,* he thought, *I'm reading too much into it.* He learned she was a divorced mother of two grown boys and worked part-time as a legal secretary. She had come down to the lounge to avoid another boring weekend of staring at the tube.

After a few more drinks, Frank began to get his courage up. His old confidence returned, and he started boasting to Leah about his savvy ability running his old tire business, how shrewd he was with investments, and how convinced he was about his political opinions. Every time Leah tried to weigh in with a comment, he seemed to ignore her or talk over her like he was on a soapbox giving a speech. After repeated attempts for nearly an hour to speak and have a conversation, she finally stood up and simply said: "I've got to go. Nice meeting you, Frank. I enjoyed the sermon." And out the door she went. *Whatever had gotten into her?* he wondered. Frank shook his head in astonishment, finished his beer, and went home.

Over the next few months, Frank tried his luck at internet dating. He joined Match.com and met Linda and Shelley. One was a hairdresser and the other a bank teller, but after the first date, neither seemed interested in him. Was he too old? Too out of shape? Was it the way he dressed? He wasn't quite sure; they hadn't said much one way or the other. Maybe he just wasn't their type. Having been out of the circuit for so long, Frank felt rather rusty and unfamiliar with the whole dating protocol.

The nights grew longer as winter settled in. The icy winds off Lake Superior rattled the window panes in Frank's farmhouse, and the snow drifted deeper across his driveway. Finding someone compatible was much more difficult than he had imagined. Dating women was not the easiest thing in the world for him, though talking to them was no big deal. He told them all about his life, his political opinions, things he believed in, books he'd read, but he couldn't find any traction. They didn't appear interested in the things he told them. In fact, they didn't appear interested in him at all.

Frank began to lose his usual swagger and slowly dissolved into a melancholy funk. In the evening, as he polished off the better part of a Bud twelve-pack, he pulled out some of his old country albums to listen to–the classics: Patsy Cline, Johnny Cash, Willie Nelson. Hearing some of the old tunes again made him think of Emily and the many good times they'd had together. He still missed her dearly, but he knew there was nothing he could change. When Patsy sang "I Fall to Pieces,"

175

Frank dropped his head between his knees and quietly wept. It had been one of Emily's favorite songs. He knew no one could ever replace Emily or even measure up to her. While she was alive, he had wanted to do so many things with her once he retired–travel to California and Alaska, take a cruise to Jamaica, visit Italy. But in a cruel, single beat, their plans had abruptly vanished–a callous stroke of bad luck.

Frank pitied himself and resented having to start over with his plans. It was certainly not the way he had pictured retirement. As he lay on the sofa listening to his old country music albums, he drifted off to sleep and dreamed of lying on a white, sandy beach surrounded by palm trees. He was rubbing tanning lotion on Emily's back and sipping a margarita. It all felt so soothing and relaxing, knowing that all the bills were paid and he had no other care in the world. Life on the beach was simple but splendid. He slept until the morning rays crept through the blinds into his den.

The next afternoon, Frank decided to stop by his old tire business in Brimley and say hello to his old crew. He missed the daily routine of going to work and having a definite purpose every day. The guys were happy to see him again and said they were sorry to hear about the loss of Emily.

"How are you adjusting to retirement?" Bob asked, handing him a cup of coffee.

"So far," Frank said, "it's not everything I was expecting, but I'm getting better at it."

Frank missed the daily chaos and hustle-bustle of the shop, especially right before and after Michigan's firearms deer season, November 15 to November 30. Everyone wanted new tires for the winter or their old snow tires mounted before the first blizzard. Most of the guys hunted, and the shop had to get along with a skeleton crew for two weeks. Frank didn't hunt himself, but someone always came through with a couple of pounds of venison for him. Frank was used to calling the shots at work, giving orders to employees, and having the last word on all work-related matters. On slower days, he looked over the tech manuals and placed orders with his tire distributor for BFGoodrich, Firestone, and Cooper brands. Working had been a decent lifestyle for a long while, but since retirement, his plans had somehow lost their footing and skidded out of control.

"Have you started dating again, or is it too soon?" Bob asked.

"Oh, I've put my toe in the water a few times, but no luck so far. I guess I'm cursed; no one wants a retread."

"Well, hang in there, Frank. The right one might come along."

It was late afternoon, and the tire shop was due to close soon. A wet, heavy snow was falling as Frank headed east on Six-Mile Road toward the Soo, just over twenty miles away. He thought he'd hit the Kewadin Casino to pass a few hours playing the slots. The beer was reasonable, and he could order an Italian grinder at the deli for supper.

As he drove through the valley of roller-coaster hills, he noticed a black car that had spun into the ditch. He pulled his truck over to see if the driver needed any help. When Frank approached the car, he saw the driver was a woman, probably in her early fifties. She unrolled her window.

"Looks like you need some help," Frank said.

"I was in way too much of a hurry coming down that hill," she said. "Don't they sand these roads anymore?"

Without answering, Frank grabbed a snow shovel from his pickup and dug the snow out from under the frame and tires.

He noted she had very little tread left on her radials.

"You sure could use a new set of snow tires. You've got no traction with these."

"Can you get me out of here?" she asked in frustration. "Or do I need to call a tow truck?"

"Just sit tight for a second; I'll have you out of here in a jiffy."

Frank walked over to a spruce tree across the ditch and snapped off several low-hanging boughs. He placed them behind the front tires and advised the woman: "Put 'er in reverse and just crawl back slowly. I'll push."

Frank got a foothold and gave the signal. She shifted into reverse and gunned it. The engine roared and spit the spruce boughs out from under the tires.

"Stop! Stop! You can't floor it like that," he said. "You have to crawl out of this ditch gradually. Here, let me behind the wheel. I'll show you."

She looked at him and reluctantly surrendered her seat. He shoveled a little more snow from under the car and repositioned the spruce branches beneath the tires. Climbing into the driver's seat, Frank shifted into reverse and eased the car back slowly until the tires got traction on the branches. The car rolled gracefully backwards back onto the pavement.

"You make that look too easy," she said, "but I'm so thankful."

"Well, I don't mind lending a hand when I can."

She looked him over quickly like she was deciding whether or not to trust him. You couldn't blame her for being wary of a complete stranger. She was well-dressed, high heels and sleek black leather gloves, and had a confident air about her.

Putting out her hand, she smiled warmly at Frank and said, "My name's Sarah, and I'd like to thank you for helping me out. I must've hit a slick patch and lost control."

"Glad I could help out, Miss. Maybe you could return the favor by going out for a drink sometime. I'm Frank, by the way."

Sarah laughed, paused, then wrote her phone number on the back of an envelope. Frank waved as she drove away.

When Frank arrived home that evening, he could not get Sarah out of his mind. He recalled his brief encounter: a lovely brunette with shoulder-length hair, her slender build, her pleasant voice—he found her quite attractive. His first impression, from the meticulous way she dressed, was she seemed like an efficient, organized, no-nonsense type of person. Yet the mischievous sparkle in her eye seemed sly and playful; her warm smile could melt a snowball.

Frank felt he'd better strike while he had his nerve up, so he picked up the kitchen phone to call her. She wouldn't go for a drink with him, but she agreed to coffee at McDonald's on Saturday morning.

At 9 a.m., he arrived at McDonald's in the Soo and found a booth just before Sarah came walking through the door. "Good morning," he said, waving her over.

"Oh, good morning, Frank."

"Since you chose the restaurant, I'm buying. Order anything you want. The sky's the limit."

She laughed and said, "You sure? I don't want to break the bank."

"Don't worry, Miss; I can handle it."

Sarah ordered a bowl of oatmeal, a toasted English muffin, and coffee. Frank ordered his usual sausage McMuffin, scrambled eggs, and pancakes, along with coffee. They picked up their orders and returned to their corner booth.

"So, Frank, tell me about yourself. What kind of work do you do besides helping stranded lady drivers?"

"Well, I've been retired for nearly a year now. I used to own a tire-and-battery shop out in Brimley. Ran that for thirty-five years until I sold it last winter. But before my feet hit the ground, my wife up and died suddenly, and here I am, still picking up the pieces."

"That's so sad," she said. "I hope you're doing all right."

"Don't mean to kill your appetite with all this, but you asked me."

"I'm kind of in the same boat," Sarah said. "My husband died in a car accident two years ago, and I'm still having a hard time accepting it, let alone talking about it with anyone."

"I hear you; I hear you. It's certainly not easy." He sipped his coffee, took a couple of bites of his sandwich and went on. "So now, I mostly work out in the yard and the garage on sunny days and take care of my investments–which takes me a lot of time because I pay very close attention to the market. I don't pay a damned broker to tell me what to invest in; I've lost more than my share doing that. No, I do my own home-work and research, and it's paid off for me handsomely, if I do say so myself. I like to follow politics, too, and all those numbskull politicians in Washington who think they're doing all of us a huge favor by their mere presence. I'd like to fire them all and start over. We'd be much better off. The political atmosphere is pure poison right now. Don't get me started on that. I'll never stop."

Sarah stared at him with her mouth open, holding a spoonful of oatmeal before her.

"What?" he asked. "Something wrong?"

"No, nothing. If you'd like to know what I do all day, I teach high school English at the senior level. I was up 'til midnight grading compositions, so I could have the weekend to myself. I really need this coffee to charge my battery this morning."

"Yeah, that's nice," Frank said absent-mindedly. "I need at least three cups in the morning to get me started. But I keep quite busy repairing things in the house, repainting some of the rooms, and maintaining my truck. I don't believe in sitting around brooding too much–it's not healthy."

Frank went on for a while talking about his yard work, books he was reading, more about politics, and then finally sports. Sarah listened politely and didn't interrupt. She thought he would eventually run out of things to say, but he didn't. He simply segued from one subject to another with hardly a breath. He moved relentlessly like a steamroller over hot, sticky pavement, never pausing for any obstacle in his path.

Sarah didn't quite know what to make of him. He seemed like an interesting man, knowledgeable, fairly intelligent, but didn't appear at all curious about her life and what she had to say. *Maybe,* she thought, *this is his way of grieving for his wife–by quickly filling in any gaps in the conversation to escape any lull, to avoid thinking entirely.* It was perhaps much more comfortable reciting certainties, familiar matters, than wrestling with unresolved personal questions.

Sarah decided to give Frank the benefit of the doubt by giving him one more try. Though he hadn't heard her say much, Frank thought she was great company and not bad looking either. He especially liked her dimples when she smiled and her warm, friendly brown eyes.

Thanksgiving was only a week away, and Frank did not want to sit home by himself watching a perennially struggling Lions team and eating a turkey TV dinner. It would be his first Thanksgiving without Emily, who always cooked the turkey and prepared all the trimmings. This year would be different, and he hoped he could get through it okay.

After several phone calls to Sarah, Frank learned she was going to be by herself at Thanksgiving as well. Her two grown children were working in California and Colorado and weren't planning to visit their mom until Christmas.

"Why don't you join me for dinner," Frank said. "I barely know how to warm up a can of soup, let alone cook a turkey. But if you give me a list, I'll pick up whatever we need. I'm sure you could talk me into peeling potatoes and lighting the candles."

"Sounds wonderful, Frank. I'd love to. But only if you'll agree to be my sous-chef and help me with the preparation."

"I'm good at following orders as long as they're not too complicated."

"Great. I'll pick up some wine and bring the music."

On Thanksgiving evening, the two of them sat down to dinner in the farmhouse kitchen. In the fields surrounding the farm, several inches of snow had fallen, ushering in the start of the holiday season. Sarah had dimmed the lights and lit two tall vanilla candles on the table. She had prepared the roast turkey, dressing, buttered carrots, asparagus, and mashed potatoes with gravy–all with Frank's assistance. Sarah poured them each a glass of chardonnay and proposed a toast.

"Here's to more pleasant days ahead of us and a short winter." They clinked glasses and took a sip.

"Well, it's been a pretty good day so far," said Frank,

"except for the Lions losing the big game again. Every year, they lay an egg. They get your hopes up all the way through the game and then find a unique way to blow it all in the end. I should've given up on this team years ago, but I still hang with 'em. I must be desperate."

"No, you're just a true sports fan. You follow your team through thick and thin."

While Sarah got up to put on a Lionel Richie CD, Frank raised his glass. "I propose a toast . . . in memory of Emily and all she meant to me. I'm sorry, maybe I shouldn't bring her up, but I miss her terribly."

Sarah took another sip of wine and said, "I know you miss her, and even though it's been over two years, I still miss Gary, too. But, at some point, we've got to move on."

Frank got up, went to the fridge, and cracked a beer. He was not particularly happy with the tone of her comment. He was doing the best he could adjusting to life without Emily, and he didn't need anyone's advice on how to cope.

Finally, Sarah felt she needed to get something off her chest, to clear the air. "You know, Frank, we've been preparing food all day long and sitting here tonight enjoying dinner and not once, not *once*, have you asked me anything about me. Aren't you the least bit curious?"

"What do you mean? I've been talking to you all day."

"Well, not exactly. You've really been talking *at* me, not *to* me. You've talked sports, politics, business, investments, and other subjects, but you've never once asked me for my personal opinion on *any* of them. Do you even care?"

"Well, sure, but . . . Didn't I ask you something about teaching English?"

"Not a word," she said.

"Well, maybe I get a little carried away sometimes," said Frank. "I don't mean anything by it. Just that I have a lot of things on my mind and need to talk about them."

"I understand, but aren't you dominating the conversation most of the time?"

"Well, for thirty-five years, I was the boss. They all came to me with questions about everything; I guess I was kind of a father figure to my crew. Maybe I know more than most people and just have a need to share my knowledge. You know, I do a lot of reading—books, newspapers, magazines. Can I help it if I have a high IQ?"

"Honestly, you know what you are, Frank? You're egotistical, and I think you're acting like a boor and a bully who just feels sorry for himself."

She began to gather her coat and things to leave when Frank said, "Now sit down for a minute. Don't go anywhere just yet. What're you trying to tell me?"

Sarah sat down again at the dining table and looked intently at Frank. "If you want to have a conversation, I would suggest that, just once, you listen closely to the other person. Look at her and give her your complete attention. That really isn't asking too much."

"I pay attention to everything you're saying even though I'm not staring at you every second."

"Yes," Sarah said, "but you barely stop to catch a breath. You drone on from one subject to another and only stop when I interrupt you. I thought you might be occasionally interested in some of my opinions and ideas and feelings about things. But you never ask. Never."

Frank felt shameful and embarrassed. No one had ever called him out like this at home or in thirty-five years of work at the shop. Maybe, Frank thought, he *was* a bully of sorts and simply wasn't aware of it. When you're the boss, you get to call the shots, and people listen. His wife, Emily, had always deferred to him in most matters. Had it been out of politeness, or was she simply trying to avoid an argument? Had she looked up to him all those years, or had he actually bullied her as well?

"The art of conversation, Frank, requires two people; otherwise, it's simply a monologue. If I try to get a word in, don't drown me out; let me speak my mind. And listen; above all things, listen carefully. Neither of us needs to dominate."

"I'm sorry, Sarah. I wasn't aware I was being such a lout. Sometimes I get carried away without knowing it."

For a moment, Sarah felt self-conscious and uncomfortable by bringing this to his attention. Despite his kindness and warmth as a person, Frank and his mindless behavior had begun to bother her to no end. *How can you have a relationship of any value,* she wondered, *if it's a one-way street?*

"What do you say we try to start all over again?" Sarah suggested. "I know that grieving takes time; I still slip in and out of old memories all the time. The way I see it, you're either here to die a little each day or to live. You have to make up your mind."

Frank wrapped his arms around her gently and looked into her eyes. "I promise you I will try to pay closer attention. Damn! Your students are sure lucky to have an English teacher like you."

Sarah smiled back at him, and for the first time, she felt grateful that they'd had a meaningful two-way conversation. Frank made a pot of coffee, and they finished the evening with a slice of homemade pumpkin pie in front of a crackling fire.

Over the next few months, Sarah often chose which restaurant to dine at, and what movie to see. Frank started asking more about her politics and what candidates she supported in the upcoming elections. He probed her opinions on various books she'd read and her take on football and basketball teams, whether she followed them closely or not. Whenever Sarah felt he was starting to go off on a tangent, monopolizing the discussion, she gently raised a hand to him, and he relented. The transition wasn't going to be easy, but he was reluctantly willing.

Retirement for Frank had been a funny thing. Just when he thought he had everything figured out, the rules of the game had changed. What had worked for him at one time no longer applied. He would either adapt or pay the price. Female companionship, for him, was more than a desirable option; it was a necessity. Without it, he felt incomplete. For Frank, learning to listen was like a fresh oil change and a new set of tires. It was good to be back on the road again.

Three Cherries

The three cherries were due to come up any moment now. Jake Powell could just feel it. Down to his last twenty bucks, he tapped the "bet" button and watched hypnotically as the cylinders revolved. They seemed to spin forever as he took a long swig of his Labatt's Blue.

For a Wednesday night, Kewadin Casino was fairly quiet and allowed him the choice of his favorite machines. Jake didn't care much for the newer animated slots—too slick and computerized for his taste. He preferred the old-fashioned Five-Card-Stud machines with the face-card images and especially favored the "fruity" slots with the cherries, oranges, and lemons. Not many of these older machines were left at the casino; they were being replaced gradually by the "cartoon" slots with all their bells, whistles, and ridiculous sound effects.

The cylinders slowed to a stop. Cherry. . . Cherry. . . Bar. Damn! Jake ordered another beer and stretched his last few dollars for a few more pulls. This tight-assed bandit was ready to pay off, and he didn't want to leave it just so some other lucky bastard could cash it in. He lit a cigarette and looked around the room, finally spotting an old friend.

"Hey, Mandy!" he shouted. She saw him waving and strolled over.

"Hi, Jake. Having much luck tonight?" She kissed him on the cheek.

"Yeah, I'm doing all right. Can you do me a big favor, sweetheart, and loan me fifty? I know you trust me."

She hesitated for a moment, then slipped him a couple of crumpled twenties from her purse. "That's the best I can do."

Jake hugged her and said, "Mandy, you're my good luck charm."

Happy to be back in the action, Jake sipped his beer and slid a twenty into the machine. To make it last longer, he played fifty cents a pull. He was somewhat lost in the mechanical whirling of the cylinders when he suddenly felt a firm grip on the back of his neck.

"Jake, old buddy, I thought I'd find you here."

"Well, Rocko, whadya know?"

"I know I want my money! And I want it now."

Rocko was a good fifty pounds heavier than Jake and had a cut-the-crap look on his face. Jake didn't want any trouble tonight, so he reached in his pocket for his last twenty.

"Here. This is all I've got. I'll square up with you on pay-day, I swear. C'mon, Rocko; lighten up."

Rocko snatched the money quickly, giving Jake the silent stare, and disappeared toward the bar. Jake blew through his remaining slot credits and headed for home. It just wasn't his night.

Around 11 p.m., Jake walked through his door with a frozen pizza and a six-pack of Busch. There was still time to watch the rest of the Red Wings game before bed. As Jake slid the pizza into the oven, his wife Jessica wandered into the kitchen. Their eight-year marriage had produced young Sarah, Jake's seven-year-old pride and joy.

"Jake, where've you been? I've been waiting up for you."

"Oh, we had to finish up that dry-walling job. It took longer than we expected."

"Did you pick up the groceries on the list I gave you?"

"Ah, sorry, hon. Ran out of time. Have to get 'em tomorrow."

"Sarah was waiting up for you, too, but got tired and went to bed. She was excited to tell you about her day at school."

"I'll go up and say goodnight to her."

~ ~ ~

Early the next morning, Jake drove to the job site a few miles out of town. He and his guys were finishing up a repair job, dry-walling and painting an older home. The hours were long and tedious, but the camaraderie with his crew more than made up for it. They joked around all day long, told stories, and played tunes on the portable radio to pass the time, but they always managed to get their work done.

For too many years, Jake had remodeled everyone's house but his own. There never seemed to be enough time or money. Maybe next winter he would redo the kitchen counters and replace the older paint-chipped cabinets. He preferred granite for the counters and hickory for the cabinets, like he had seen in some of the newer log homes being built just outside of town. They would be expensive, but he would try to negotiate a good deal. Jessica wanted the hardwood floor resanded and finished as well as a new shower installed to replace the dilapidated one upstairs. And if they expected Sarah to be a good student in school, she would need a computer in her room. He promised Jessica he would start on the renovations as soon as he could, if the money was there.

By 6 p.m., Jake and the crew finished work for the day and headed back into town. Jake thought about driving straight home, but he decided to stop at the casino for a quick beer with the boys. One drink followed another, and soon he forgot about going home or even calling Jessica. He enjoyed the festive excitement of the casino, the parade of brilliant colors before him. The possibility of hitting a big winner stimulated him and made him forget the long workday.

Praying for a winner, he pumped the slots until his money was gone. He had the same lousy luck that night and the night after that. Jake owed more money to more people and tried to avoid them any way he could as he wandered around the smoky casino. The musical hum of the machines and the dazzling flash of the lights mesmerized him. His luck was due to change any moment; he just sensed it. But Jake also knew his bank account was exhausted and he needed to catch up on his bills.

Rummaging through his closet one weekend, he had come across his old Epiphone flattop guitar that he used to play as a teenager. Though he felt somewhat sentimental about it, he hadn't played it in years. The only reason he'd kept the guitar was because Sarah had talked about someday taking lessons. The local Swap Shop gave him a hundred bucks for it, enough to get him through this rough patch. As he told himself, he could always buy it back.

The following week, on a Thursday night, the three cherries finally lined up, and Jake was twelve hundred dollars richer. He celebrated by paying off most of the people he had borrowed money from and brought home a bucket of KFC chicken and a Little Caesar's pizza, Chicago-style. The rest of the money went to his wife to pay down the bills.

Jake found it odd and disappointing that Jessica simply took it all in stride. She seemed neither excited nor relieved at his good fortune. It had not fazed her in the least. Instead, she had a distant, puzzled look about her, as if she were not really in the same room as him, but in some faraway dream.

"Is this the way we're always going to live?" she finally asked. "Feast or famine? Paycheck to paycheck? You know, I'm really getting sick of this."

"Jessica, I thought you'd be happy that we finally caught a break."

"I was hoping you could change, but now, I'm not so sure. You've dipped into Sarah's college fund at the bank; we have no money to fix up the car; you've even spent my emergency fund in the coffee can."

"I'll pay it all back, I swear. Every cent of it." Jake turned away and stared out the window, disgusted with himself.

"How do you expect me to trust you anymore? I just don't know what to do."

Jessica began to sob quietly. Jake took her in his arms and held her closely. In a whisper, he said, "I am so sorry I've done this to you."

"Daddy?" There was a small voice at the edge of the room.

"Yes, dear. What are you doing up so late?"

"I'm thirsty. Can I have a drink of water?"

"Sure, honey," Jake said and watched his daughter stumble to the sink and pick up a glass. After she drank some water, Sarah rubbed the sleep out of her eyes. "Daddy, are you coming to my soccer game after work tomorrow? I'm going to score a goal for you."

Looking at Jessica and Sarah, Jake said, "I'm going to try hard from now on . . . for both of you. You have to trust me one more time. Of course, I'm coming to your game." Jake picked Sarah up and kissed her on the cheek.

Jessica looked into his eyes and wanted to believe him, but she wasn't so sure. She'd been disappointed too many times in the past. Jake, for his part, regretted having behaved so deceptively. This time, he promised, things would be different. They would have to be. He knew he had too much to lose.

~ ~ ~

For the next several weeks, Jake stayed away from the casino. He still owed money to people, including Rocko, and needed to pay them up soon. After work, he came straight home and often went shopping at the supermarket with Jessica and Sarah. But it wasn't easy for him. He missed having a few drinks after work with his buddies and trying his luck at the slots. Jessica was happy he had changed his ways and complimented him.

After a month's time, Jake had an itch to stop by the Kewadin for just a short time. It was good to see old friends again after his short hiatus. They treated him like a long-lost soldier. "Jake, where've you been? Haven't seen you in such a long while." It was like being welcomed home after an exile. Soon, he was stopping there two or three nights a week.

One Friday night, when Jake arrived home after 10 p.m., the house was silent and empty. He found a letter on the kitchen table from Jessica.

> Dear Jake,
>
> Sarah and I have left and moved in with my folks in Pickford. I can't take your lying and gambling any longer. I thought you had truly changed, but the truth is I don't think you can. I guess you must love the gambling life more than you love us. I refuse to wait around any longer for you to get your life together, so I'm moving on. I will be filing divorce papers as soon

as I can get my bearings. I'm sorry, but we gave it a good try.

Love,

Jessica

Jake was stunned. He hadn't seen this coming. He tried calling Jessica at her parents' place in Pickford, but she wouldn't speak to him. Though she was only twenty miles away, Jessica left word through her mother for Jake to stay away and not bother them. *Maybe she needs her space for a while*, Jake thought. *She'll miss me before long. She'll be back soon.*

Being alone, he felt, might not be so bad. No questions to answer if he came in late, no need to tell little white lies, more time to spend with his friends. This could be a stroke of luck for him.

That Saturday night, Jake stopped by the casino again. He sat down at the bar and ordered a Blue to ease into the evening. Halfway through his beer, a familiar figure sat down on the stool next to him.

"Wasn't expecting to see you here tonight, Jake. You'll never guess what I want from you."

"Easy now, Rocko. You want your 500, I know. And I plan to pay you, but things are a little tight right now."

"Oh, yeah," said Rocko. "Tell you what. I'll give you two more hours to cough up my money, and that's it. Final. You don't want to upset me, Jake; it wouldn't be healthy for you. Trust me." And he disappeared into the crowd.

Jake finished his beer and walked through the Paradise Room, talking to friends for a short-term loan to pay Rocko off. Knowing his reputation for borrowing money, nobody would lend him a cent. So Jake approached one of the fruity slots that had given him good luck recently and invested two twenties. Just before his credits ran out, he struck two cherries and a wild card for 150 bucks. Instead of walking away with his winnings, Jake kept pumping the machine, knowing it was starting to heat up. For the next hour, he was up 200, then before long, down to his last ten dollars. In one spin, he was flat broke again.

Jake hustled out a side door, hoping to avoid Rocko. Marching to the far end of the darkened parking lot, Jake found his Ford pickup. The front windshield had been bashed in, as if by a heavy pipe or a baseball bat. All four tires had been severely slashed. Jake knew right away it was a warning from Rocko. He trudged back to the casino and called a wrecker.

After a couple of weeks, Jake's carefree lifestyle was losing its appeal. The house felt quiet and deserted when he came home—total darkness, no voices, no sign of life. Jake made his own breakfast and dinner and let the dishes stack up as long as possible. A pile of empty pizza boxes grew taller in the corner. The stillness every night was beginning to drive him mad. Every evening he watched sports and old movies until he fell asleep, lost in an array of bags and wrappers from Taco Bell and McDonald's. His life seemed to be descending into a monotonous sameness. He wore the same jeans, red sweatshirt, and work boots every day without changing. What was the point anymore? Having lost all self-respect, Jake was ashamed of himself and the direction he was headed.

Again, one night, he tried phoning Jessica, but she was sleeping. It was nearly midnight. He left a message for her to please call him. In bed, he lay awake thinking of why Jessica had left him. She'd lost trust in him; she'd lost respect for him. And he knew he deserved it. He had never told her the truth about his gambling debts. Small lies to cover up had led to bigger lies. His dishonesty with her, and with himself, had tripped him up time and time again. The end game, he decided, was clearly up. If Jake didn't clean up his act soon, he stood to lose both Jessica and Sarah—the only ones who really mattered to him. He wondered how he could regain her trust and respect, her belief in him.

Jake had always admired his younger brother Jeremy for earning his electrician's license and working for himself. It hadn't been easy for Jeremy. He had worked as a low-paid apprentice for many long hours before testing for his license. But it had been worth it in the long run; he was now working in Marquette at a high-paying job. He had the financial security Jake could only envy.

Jake soon decided he would study for his builder's license, as Jessica had often encouraged, and not put it off any longer. A license would enable him to legally contract for residential construction. He could do away with all the short-term drywall work and questionable remodeling jobs. He could grow his income by building new homes instead of always repairing old ones.

The next morning, Jessica returned his call early, before Jake left for work.

"I need you back home here, Jessica. I miss you and Sarah badly. Could you possibly reconsider before calling that lawyer?"

"I gave you a fair chance, Jake, and you blew it. How do expect me ever to trust you to do what you promise?"

"Listen," Jake pleaded, "you name the price. Anything you want. Just . . . please come back."

Jessica paused a moment, sniffled, and quietly blew her nose. Jake waited for an answer. She did not want to wade through another round of broken promises; she needed a guarantee.

"I'll tell you what," she said, "we'll come back, on one condition. I'll do all the business books, pay the bills, and take care of all the money. After work, you come straight home. No casino anymore."

"Whatever you want," Jake said.

"And if I ever hear of you gambling again, I am out of there for good. You understand? I love you, Jake, but I'll never go through this BS with you again."

When Jessica and Sarah returned, they had been away for several weeks. Jake's reunion with them was both happy and tearful. In addition to her new bookkeeping responsibilities, Jessica found a part-time afternoon job as a supermarket cashier while Sarah was at school. Jake tried to engage in more activities with his family, taking them out for ice cream or pizza occasionally, or to the beach on weekends. They started spending more time in the summer at the Powell camp in Hessel that his father had built. Sarah especially enjoyed the marshmallow roasting around the campfire. His days were so busy there seemed to be less time for Jake even to think of the casino.

With Jessica doing the books, they slowly paid off Jake's gambling debts and started putting some money into fixing up the house. Then they cleared the many scattered backyard toys and, in a sunny patch, planted a small garden. After a fresh load of topsoil and compost was brought in, they sowed a variety of green peppers, tomatoes, and cucumbers.

As the summer months stretched out, the tiny plants grew and prospered, filling the backyard with a palette of colorful vegetables. Even little Sarah helped tend the garden, plucking the nasty weeds wherever they sprouted. On weekends, Jake was soon finding time to work on some of his own home repair projects. He thought about gambling from time to time and missed the excitement, but the trade-off had been the better bet for him.

Jake's relationship, like the garden, needed to be watered, weeded, and fertilized. In time, the garden became a labor of love for him, and he was expecting an abundant harvest.

Shoehorn

First, the wedding was on; then it was off. Sam was reluctant to get married, but Terri had insisted. If he expected her to stick around for long, he knew he'd have to go through with it. They had been dating for only a year, and Sam wanted to be sure he'd made the right choice. But, at the same time, he didn't want to lose Terri.

Sam's family had broken up when he was a young teenager. His older brother, Tony, had lasted for nearly five years before his relationship dissolved. It was no wonder Sam was so cautious about jumping in with both feet. Terri, on the other hand, reminded him that being in their late twenties, time was moving on—especially if they were planning to start a family. She wanted two to three kids, preferably two girls and a boy; Sam hadn't really thought about it one way or the other.

For nearly three years, Sam had worked as manager of Benson's Shoes at the local mall in Traverse City. The hours were long and the salary only average, but he was hoping to work his way up in the company by respectfully paying his dues and running a profitable store.

The company required him to work weekends and several evenings and to fill in whenever an employee didn't show up. By saving a few dollars each paycheck and driving a ten-year-old Chevy, Sam hoped to put away enough money for a down payment on a modest house, or maybe a winter vacation to the Caribbean. He hadn't taken a real vacation since he'd become the manager, and he knew he needed one soon. His anxieties and frustrations over work were piling up.

Sam and Terri had met each other at a local Holiday Inn lounge. She had caught his eye one night on the dance floor, wearing a short strapless black dress. Though he didn't dance much himself, Sam still enjoyed the familiar pulse of the music and the lounge's dimmed down atmosphere. When Terri had come up to the bar to refresh her drink, Sam had complimented her looks and offered to buy her a drink. By the end of the night, she'd given him her phone number.

A few years earlier, Terri had gone to school to become a hairdresser. Since moving to Traverse City from Cheboygan, she had built up a steady clientele of loyal customers. She liked to dance and party with her friends, but she couldn't seem to find a good relationship. The one-night stands were growing old; she wanted to meet someone more reliable she could trust, somebody with a plan for the future. She wanted no more to do with any good-looking, sweet-talking, alcoholic party boys who were looking for only a one-night hookup. Terri was ready to settle down.

For a year, Sam and Terri dated. They went out to dinner, the movies, and for drinks afterward. Terri liked Sam's dry sense of humor and his quiet, unassuming manner. One evening at her apartment, she caught him off guard.

"We've known each other for quite some time now, Sam, and we get along so well. Have you ever . . . thought about getting married?"

"Well," he stammered, "I haven't really thought much about it. We have a good thing going now. Maybe we should give it some time to grow."

"I'm nearly thirty, Sam, and if I'm ever going to have children, I can't wait too much longer. If you've got cold feet, I might have to think about moving on before long."

Sam hadn't seen that coming. *Is she giving me an ultimatum?* he wondered. "You mean find somebody else? Seriously? Now don't go rushing into things. Give me a few days to think this over."

Sex with Terri was satisfying but not great. She seemed preoccupied, like she was simply checking something off her daily to-do list. Perhaps her mind was focused on something else, like picking out furniture or measuring for carpet; who knew?

The next day at the shoe store, Sam worked from ten in the morning to nine at night. By then, he was so tired he couldn't think straight. He was putting shoes back in the wrong boxes, mixing up sizes, and ringing up the wrong prices at the cash register. With Terri's demands on his mind, he was having trouble sleeping; he felt backed into a corner with very few options. And she was insisting on an answer soon.

If Sam waited to get married, she would probably leave him, unless . . . she was bluffing. He couldn't be totally sure. If she left to find someone more willing, he would have to start over, and that would be hard on him. The two of them were quite fond of each other, but Sam didn't feel a deep love between them. That would come in time, he felt, if they worked at it.

Terri, he had learned, had expensive taste for a shoe salesman's salary. She liked to dine at the finest restaurants in town and buy her clothes at the most fashionable boutiques. She had a disarming way of smiling at him and pouting when she wanted things her way. To satisfy her and avoid a bitter argument, he would usually agree with her preferences and say something like, "Oh, all right, that's fine." A small sacrifice on his part, it usually diffused the situation and gave him peace of mind.

When Terri would hear a good band was coming to Detroit, she would often ask him to buy concert tickets for the show at Pine Knob. Between a weekend hotel, tickets, restaurants, and driving expenses, his biweekly check was being stretched to the limit. But Sam wanted to make her happy, so he rarely turned her down.

Getting married would be a game changer for Sam, a turning point, a commitment to one person for the balance of his life. He was excited by the opportunity, but scared to death by the finality of it all. Still, it seemed if he hesitated, a chapter in his life would be closing for good; he would have to turn the page.

The following Monday, Sam and Terri agreed to meet for lunch at a small café on Garfield. When Sam walked in, Terri had a pensive look and an air of no surrender. She appeared to have played her last card and didn't want a redeal. He didn't want to keep her in suspense any longer so he simply said, "I'll do it." She let out a giddy scream of excitement, hugged him, and smiled happily with a sense of relief. Not wasting any time, Terri got right to the point.

"Of course, I've already picked out an engagement ring," she said breathlessly. "I know how you hate to shop. It is so beautiful, but I know it's worth it. You only get married once in your life."

"Well, since I'm sitting down now, tell me what this little gem is going to cost."

"The jeweler says they were originally asking $8,000, but they've discounted it to only $6,000, and we can make payments of under $300 a month."

Sam's eyes widened. He swallowed hard and took a deep breath, trying not to overreact. Somehow, he thought, they would find a way to afford it. At the same time, he wondered if it would be wiser to put the bulk of that $6,000 toward a down payment on a house. As he quickly learned, Terri would not even consider it. More than anything, and as a sign of his devotion to her, she wanted the ring.

As the days passed and their wedding plans came together, a number of unforeseen problems developed. Sam favored a smaller, more intimate wedding with just family members and close friends. Terri dreamt of a big blowout affair with 300 wedding guests at an upscale hotel. Sam wanted a honeymoon of hiking and camping in the Upper Peninsula. Terri had her heart set on a wedding cruise to Jamaica. And just one other thing: she no longer wished to rent but insisted on shopping for a house to buy on the west side of Traverse City, something in the modest range of $175,000 to $200,000.

The wedding plans seemed to take on a life of their own. Terri reveled in the details of wedding gowns, bridesmaids, flowers for the church, table settings, and decorations. Sam's input was reduced to the minimum: pick three groomsmen and a best man, and try to be on time for the ceremony. They booked the country club for the reception and a local blues band for the entertainment.

Expenses were running higher than expected, and Sam and Terri would have to finance the bulk of it. Both sets of parents were a little strapped for funds and could only help out so much. Terri's father was a bricklayer and her mother a clerk at a downtown department store, so they were hoping for a backyard wedding with a big canopy tent. Perhaps Uncle Tony could play his guitar and bring his karaoke machine. But Terri wouldn't even discuss the suggestion; it was light years away from her vision.

Both of Sam's parents were schoolteachers, though his mother had recently been laid off. As long as Sam's wedding arrangements were within his means, they were happy to support him with a reasonable contribution. They believed in the less-said-the-better policy when it came to interfering in their son's relationship and didn't ask for too many particulars.

Several weeks after the wedding, when the bills started rolling in, Sam sat down one night at the kitchen table to sort out their expenses. After mortgage payments, heat and utility bills, food, and car expenses, there was nothing left over. They would have to start living on a budget or find higher-paying jobs. The numbers just didn't add up the way he would have liked.

But Terri was stubborn. She did not feel like cutting back on anything, especially not restaurants or vacations. A young married couple, after all, was entitled to a few extra perks. Terri maxed out their credit limit on the Visa card and bought furniture that offered an easy monthly payment plan. Sam thought they should cook more meals at home, but she preferred the pleasures of eating out regularly.

Terri was also not totally pleased with the two-bedroom ranch they had settled for ten miles out of town. However, the homes in town were much too pricey, and living in a tiny apartment was out of the question.

Terri talked about starting a family soon, but Sam wanted to get their finances in better order first. Children, loveable as they were, would be a major expense, in terms of both money and time. He was already working fifty hours a week at the mall shoe store and wanted to ask for a raise. The money Terri earned as a hairdresser was deposited in a separate account. She thought of it as her mad money, for personal purchases, not to pay bills with. Sam did not like this arrangement, but he had not questioned her about it. Anytime he asked her to help out more with the monthly bills, she would only get flustered and abruptly leave the room. So, to keep the peace in their household, he let her win most of their disagreements.

After six months of marriage, the luster of their relationship had begun to fade. Their nights out at the movies and in restaurants were less frequent. With both of them working a full schedule, little time or energy was left at the end of the day. Barely enough time to change clothes, warm up some frozen dinners, and doze off in front of the TV.

One evening, as they were getting ready for bed, Terri felt she had to say what was bothering her. "We never go out anymore, Sam, like we used to. We just stay home every night."

"We can't afford it anymore. In case you hadn't noticed, I can barely pay the bills every month."

"I know, but I'm getting bored. I want to have more fun in my life. Let's fly out to Las Vegas for a few days. Let's go somewhere."

"I would really love to," Sam said in disbelief, "but we just don't have the money. I can't put any more on our charge cards; they're nearly maxed out again."

But Terri wasn't really listening. Why, she wondered, does everything have to be so logical and practical? We should follow our passion, go with our gut instinct. Things will work themselves out. They always do.

The stresses of work and marriage were mounting in Sam's head. He wasn't eating well or sleeping. At work, he looked exhausted. Before long, he found himself wandering into the mall pub after work to have a few unwinding drinks with friends. Dinner soon became a bag of pretzels and a bowl of beer nuts.

Sunday was the only day Sam could catch up with his yard work. He enjoyed the change of pace and being outdoors—mowing the grass and planting a few trees and bushes. Terri didn't particularly like housework. She wished they could afford to hire a cleaning person to wash the dishes, vacuum the carpets, and do the laundry. So the housework piled up, and their tempers began to fray. Sam tried to help out where he could, but he hesitated to criticize Terri because he didn't want to risk another full-blown argument. Things had grown tense enough as it was.

It wasn't long before Terri wasn't coming home right after work. Her friends asked her to join them at happy hour down at Union Street. Drinking and laughing with friends for a few hours seemed much more appealing to her than going home, watching TV, and arguing.

Back in January, the company had given Sam a 2 percent raise, just enough to keep up with inflation. When his bills began to get away from him, he asked the company for a 10 percent raise, but they refused. So Sam decided to be proactive and take charge of things by slipping a few dollars out of the cash register each week. At first, it was just $25 a week; soon it was up to $50, several nights a week. He began to write up more over-rings to account for the shortages. At store closing time, he underreported the day's totals by a few dollars and made the nightly bank deposit. As manager, he felt it was time he called the shots.

Less than two months later, Sam's head office noticed the pattern of falling weekly sales and looked into the matter. They became suspicious and, working with local police, discreetly mounted a hidden camera over the cash register area.

To himself, Sam justified the theft. He had worked long hours for the company, year after year, and was being greatly underpaid. The Benson Shoe Company probably made millions in profits, so what was a few dollars here or there? Besides, they hadn't provided him with a paid vacation in three years. It was his due compensation. Sam didn't mention a word about the ploy to his wife; that would only complicate matters. But to make ends meet, he knew it was his only way out of a tight situation.

When the police appeared at the shoe store one day, they took Sam straight to jail. He didn't resist and almost welcomed the arrest. He was charged with embezzlement and, after the court trial, was ordered to serve five to seven years in the state penitentiary. With good behavior, he could expect to be paroled in two to three years.

After the news of Sam's arrest became public, Terri felt humiliated and angry at him for doing such a thoughtless thing to her. Before he left for prison, she demanded a divorce. She was not about to put her life on hold and wait until he was free. In an odd sort of way, Sam felt a sense of great relief, an indescribable burden having been lifted from his shoulders.

Within a few months of being arrested, Sam fell behind on his house payments, and the bank foreclosed. It would be several years before he finished paying off the engagement ring. He thought, perhaps, he should file for bankruptcy, but he hesitated because he thought he would lose his credit for several years. When it was all over and he had served his time, Sam planned to go out west. The best thing, he felt, was to get out of Dodge for a change, to straighten things out and start fresh.

The last he heard, Terri had hooked up with a pharmaceutical salesman and moved to Chicago. Sam hoped the poor man had a few spare Valiums tucked away in his samples. Just in case.

A Watchman's Log

Sept. 15, 2018: My son and daughter, Joseph and Sofia, thought it would be a good idea for me to make a tape recording every so often of what's going on in my life and in my head. It's meant to be a personal record of everyday thoughts and activities so they will remember what kind of a guy their father was. When I'm gone, they're free to share these tapes with my good friends, if they're interested. This makes me feel like Studs Terkel, talking to myself, but I'll give it a try.

At eighty-two, I think I forget more things than I remember. Names, dental appointments, birthdays–if I don't write them down, they are toast. Just as well sometimes; I like being busy, but not frantic. If I play this age thing the right way, they don't hold my feet to the fire. They almost expect an old guy like me to forget things. Now, there was a point I was going to make . . . .

Sept. 24, 2018: First, a bit of history. My wife, Linda, and I bought this little house fifty-five years ago and raised a son and a daughter. It's here on the lower St. Mary's River, just south of the Soo's city limits. We could see the freighters out back, steaming up-bound and down-bound, which reminds me of my past years of working on the lakes.

I retired as a watchman seventeen years ago and sailed for over forty years on fifteen different Great Lakes freighters. Started out as a deckhand and worked my way up the hawsepipe to deck watch, then wheelsman, and finally settled in as watchman. I mainly worked the 4-to-8 shift with the first mate and, for the most part, had a great life out there. Lonely at times, being away from family for months at a stretch, but it was good money, and I loved every season on the Great Lakes–the storms, the sunsets, the great expanse of blue water, the wind and waves. It made me feel alive and thankful that I wasn't stuck working somewhere behind a desk in some windowless office.

Sept. 30, 2018: Linda passed away five years ago, and I've been on my own ever since. To have her near me, I've kept her ashes in a carved mahogany box on the mantle; it comforts me. We'd been married over fifty years and raised a family here in the Soo. She never liked me working on the boats for so many years, the long separations, although our reunions were very special. Since I was gone so often, Linda bore the brunt of raising our family. My son and daughter didn't see much of me during the year, except at Christmas sometimes and all winter long. Every spring, I left again for a new season on the boats. I often wonder how much I missed.

Oct. 2, 2018: For anyone hearing this, long after I'm gone, I guess I should make it official. My name is Marco Barcelli, born in Ishpeming in 1936. My father was an iron ore miner; his father and grandfather were stone masons from Italy, the old country. I might have followed in my father's footsteps, but I'm a little claustrophobic and would have never survived in underground tunnels no matter how good the pay. I preferred to be out in the open air where there's sunshine and blue water. That's why I was attracted to the big 600-foot ore freighters that loaded at the docks in Marquette. Once I had a taste of the boats and the lakes, I knew I'd found a life I could love. The camaraderie of the crewmembers, the great food, good money, sailing through the four seasons on the lakes–there's plenty to like.

Oct. 5, 2018: I can't seem to get it off my mind today. I feel bad abandoning my family—my wife and kids—at a time when they needed me most. I should have been there and not working on the lakes, but I can't change that now. Joe and Sofia, I hope you can forgive me for that; I feel terrible that I let you and your mother down. I should have been with you growing up—attending your sports games, school plays, helping you with your homework. Maybe I seemed more like a visiting uncle to you than an actual father. I'm sorry. A man almost loses his right to make family decisions when he's gone most of the year. Please forgive me.

Oct. 9, 2018: I met my wife, Linda, at a bowling alley in Marquette. She was the pinsetter. A couple of years later, we married, and she attended NMU and earned her teaching certificate in history. We eventually moved to the Soo so she could teach at the middle school. Meanwhile, I got my Merchant Marine card and found work as a deckhand on the freighters. There were plenty of jobs available on the boats back in the '60s. They've pretty much dried up since then. Only a handful of 1000-footers still sailing, probably due to so much imported steel today. But that was shipping's heyday in the U.S.

Oct. 12, 2018: I live on a small monthly pension from the boats and my Social Security. My house is paid off, so I mostly have to pay for just the bills–the heat, cable, and taxes. I'm not rolling in dough, but I'm holding my own. There are plenty of ways I've discovered to save money. I keep the heat in the wintertime down to 62 degrees, wear long underwear all winter, and keep a sweater and a fleece on during the colder months. I spend very little in restaurants and prefer to cook my own meals anyway. I've become quite a chef in my old age. My specialties are ham-and-bean soup, lasagna, and bacon cheeseburgers. What? You expect me to live on salads?

Oct. 22, 2018: Tom, a retired guy younger than myself, delivers lunch to me every day from Meals-On-Wheels. He stops by sometimes after his deliveries for a few games of cribbage and to share a little town gossip. I think Tom's trying to hit on one of his female clients; he visits her frequently for coffee and homemade cinnamon rolls. I keep asking him when he's going to pop the question, but he won't answer me.

Otherwise, the only thing that gets me out of the house every week is tennis. I play twice a week up at the college with a group of folks who are a few years younger than me. I can't race around the court much anymore, but I'm deadly at the net. I'm usually quick enough to catch any low-flying returns in my vicinity. After tennis, we head out to a bar downtown for beers and burgers and tell a few stories. We know how to have a good time. It's my main social life. Well, OK, my only social life.

Oct. 29, 2018: Some people probably think I'm a curmudgeon or a loner the way I'm holed up in this house for days at a time. But I'm perfectly comfortable living alone, although it's taken some major adjustment since my wife died. I have plenty of good books to read, mostly history and biographies. In the summer, I split wood for the fireplace; in the winter, I snow-blow the driveway and shovel the steps. At my age, I've slowed down my pace considerably, but I try to stay active. In the morning and evening, I walk my dog, Lady, around the neighborhood. Then I watch a little politics on TV to try to keep up with all the shenanigans in Washington. After dinner, I treat myself to a couple of shots of Jack Daniels on the rocks. It's one of my few vices, and I have no intention of giving it up.

Nov. 2, 2018: I'm not quite sure what's come over me lately. Some days I feel good about myself; on others, I want to throw in the towel. There's almost no reason to get out of bed in the morning. Nothing is going right for me anymore. One day is the same as the next. What's the point anymore? Time is weighing heavier on me, and I can't look at the endless days on the calendar anymore. There must be some way out of this misery. This is just not like me.

Nov. 5, 2018: This is sometimes a sad part of the year for me with Thanksgiving and Christmas coming up. I think of many family gatherings when the kids were growing up, the golden roast turkey coming out of the oven, decorating the Christmas tree. It all went by so fast, and now I have only faded photographs and warm memories. It's not quite enough. It ought to last longer than it does.

Too many of the holidays were spent aboard ship. I regret being away from my family on so many of those occasions. But as a watchman on the Great Lakes freighters, it was my responsibility as breadwinner. My kids grew up without a father around for eight months out of the year. That's the price we paid for such an arrangement, but I'm not sure how I could have done things differently. Water under the bridge now.

Nov. 15, 2018: The snow is back again, four or five inches yesterday. I don't mind winter, though. The house is warm enough with the fireplace blazing, and I seem to get a lot more reading done. You have to like U.P. winters to live here. They come early in November and don't leave until late in April. It's a very contemplative time of year.

In the winter, you tend to think back over your life–the milestones, some of the happier times with family and friends, even your regrets and disappointments, things that didn't turn out as you'd hoped. Sometimes, I wish I'd have been around more often when Linda needed me, when my son and daughter were growing up. Maybe I'd have been closer to them, and maybe they would know me better. Did I really have to spend forty years of my life working on the boats? Couldn't I have found some kind of work closer to home? Too late. I'll never know the answer. But I do think about it all the time and wonder. Then again, maybe I'm just fooling myself, out of a sense of guilt. Truth is, I loved working on the lakes.

Nov. 30, 2018: If it weren't for crank calls, scams, and junk mail, my life would be dull and colorless. Why just this morning I received a call from "the IRS." A guy on the phone said I was behind in my taxes and needed to send out a check immediately, or a warrant for my arrest would be issued. A few days later, I got a call from a very nervous fellow who claimed my grandson was in jail and needed bail money. I told him to keep the youngster in the slammer until he straightens out. Might be good for him. The truth is, I don't have any grandsons, only a couple of granddaughters, including one who works for the IRS.

Another day, I had a call from someone who claimed I had won a "fabulous Caribbean vacation." He congratulated me enthusiastically and said all he needed was my Visa number for a hotel deposit. I don't even like hot, humid weather and would never lie on a sandy beach for more than two minutes. That would be misery. Unless perhaps a beautiful native girl was fanning me with a palm leaf and plying me with margaritas.

My daily junk mail usually includes pleas for me to support polar bears, honey bees, the Humane Society, the ACLU, marijuana reform, and a wide assortment of politicians. I'm led to believe many of these worthwhile causes will fail immediately if I neglect to send in a generous contribution today. I've stopped sending contributions to anyone because they have all passed my name around to every fly-by-night fundraising organization in the country. I must be an easy mark, but I can barely keep up with my own bills and expenses. Maybe I should be playing the lottery or the slots at the casino more often. I would sure appreciate a few pennies from heaven.

Dec. 15, 2018: My part-time housekeeper, Laura, comes by the house several days a week to check on me and do a few chores like dishwashing and vacuuming. For a woman in her early thirties, she's not bad looking. I've been trying to arrange a date with her for weeks, but she's been playing hard-to-get.

My son, Joseph, and my daughter, Sofia, come up from downstate to visit me regularly. We tell old stories of when they were growing up and browse through family photo albums. The photos recorded so many wonderful moments I'd forgotten. I'm very grateful for them.

My kids want me to move downstate where they are, but I like it here in the U.P. and want to stay. This is home to me. What would I ever do down there with all the crowds of people and the maddening traffic? All my friends, the few remaining, are living here.

I hope I've made it very clear to Joe and Sofia that if I ever come down with cancer or Alzheimer's or something like that, I never want to be placed in a nursing home or any kind of warehouse institution. With the help of a doctor to administer pain meds, I prefer to live at home comfortably until I drift away, hopefully with my son and daughter nearby. I've led a reasonably happy and challenging life and would be much more content at home in my final days than in a cold, sterile hospital room. I'm calling the shots on this one.

Jan. 1, 2019: I made it through New Year's Eve, but just barely. I was by myself last night, feeling very lonely. I'm not proud of what I did, and I'm not entirely sure why. But I came home from the hardware store with a twenty-five-foot length of heavy rope and, just before midnight, I strung it over a beam in the living room, stood on a chair, and tightened the noose around my neck. Maybe I just wanted a way out of my loneliness and despair. As the days pass by, I think of Linda and miss her terribly; it's so painful some days, I feel I can't go on. I have nothing to live for. But then, standing on that chair, ready to leap, I thought of Joe and Sofia. I love them dearly and thought about them having to deal with my suicide and how much pain and shame it might cause them; I couldn't do that to them; it's not how I want to be remembered.

Jan. 3, 2019: Had a pleasant visit today with a couple of Jehovah's Witnesses who knocked at my door. I invited them inside for coffee to warm up a bit, and they proceeded to tell me their views of the world, the present one as well as the one to come. I found it interesting but couldn't quite buy it. They feel I should be joyful that when the world ends soon, the faithful ones will all be reunited with their long-lost friends and relatives. If I was among them, I would be spending eternity with all these folks, including people I never got along with, bosses I couldn't stand, and politicians who drove me crazy. The whole proposal didn't sound all that appealing to me in the long run. Hopefully, we'll have other options. Personally, I'd be perfectly content if there was no afterlife. Life is rich enough and long enough as it is without trying to stretch it out forever. Can I get an amen?

Jan. 28, 2019: When I was a teenager, in Ishpeming, I learned to ski-jump off Suicide Hill. A few of my friends were jumping and dared me to give it a try. Butterflies and queasiness don't even begin to describe the raw nervousness that ran through my body as I climbed up to that jumping platform. My friends coached me on leaning forward and angling my skis, but when I finally sprang off the end of that jump, with only the wide world of nothing below me, I thought it would be my final breath on this earth. Only two thin wooden slats between me and total oblivion. I made the telemark landing as instructed but tumbled several times down the hill, luckily with no broken body parts. After that experience, there wasn't much in life that ever made me nervous again. Sometimes, when it comes down to confronting your fears or being called "chicken shit" by your friends, the choice becomes crystal clear.

Feb. 14, 2019: It's Valentine's Day today, and I bought a red rose and laid it in front of Linda's picture on the mantle. She looks so beautiful in that picture that was taken right after we were married, smiling down at me so warmly, her long auburn hair cascading over her bare shoulders. I still love her and miss her so much and wish I'd told her more often when I had the chance.

March 3, 2019: On some Fridays, my friend Lenny picks me up for the fish fry at the VFW or sometimes for a pasty down at the Legion. Lenny is ten years younger than me and still drives; I surrendered my driver's license about five years ago after absent-mindedly running through a couple of red lights and nearly running over a pedestrian. My eyes are going little by little. Anyway, Lenny and I play a little cribbage or maybe a game of pool while we're sipping our beers. Sooner or later, the guys get around to talking about war stories. I can't say too much because it brings back too many horrible memories. I signed up and served my time in Nam for my country, and I'm glad I did it, but I hated that war. At first, I was gung-ho about slaughtering "the gooks," the North Vietnamese soldiers, our mortal enemies. Then after two of my buddies were killed in a gruesome way and I understood more about the U.S. involvement in the war, I turned against it. The war was worthless, what it did to all of us–the soldiers and the country back home. Nothing good ever came of it, and I can't keep reliving the past. Hopefully, we'll be more careful about getting ourselves into any more wars in the future.

They're damn near impossible to get out of.

March 21, 2019: To Joe and Sofia: Keep in mind what I said about nursing homes and hospitals. I prefer to stay as far away from them as possible. It's nothing personal, just that when my time comes, I'd be much happier in a familiar place like my own home. I'm starting to sound like Woody Allen: "I'm not afraid of death. I just don't want to be there when it happens."

As for me, I seem to be on a more even keel lately. I realize that even though I wasn't there much of the time while you were growing up, I can still be an example to both of you: to never take the easy way out; to work through difficult personal issues; to stay upbeat about life as much as possible. I'm not completely out of the woods myself by any means, but I've been getting a little help regularly down at the clinic. I'll be fine.

For many years, I've always wanted to go to Italy, where my grandparents were raised. My grandfather told me so many wonderful stories about the old country when he was growing up. I had promised your mother a trip there someday, but we never made it in time. So when I finally slip away, I'm leaving enough money for your families to travel to Florence, Italy. It's my last wish for all of you, and I know you'll come through. When you arrive there, spread my ashes along with your mother's under the Tuscan sun. If we're going to spend eternity together somewhere, we'd like to be warm for a change. *Con amore, arrivederci.*

~ ~ ~

After the service, Joe and Sofia returned with their father's ashes to his house on the river. They sat by the fireplace and listened once more to his recent recordings.

"Italy?" Sofia mused. "I think he's serious."

The Bait Pile

When the war in Europe finally ended, and Hitler was defeated, Ethan Powell returned to the States and built a rustic cabin in the deep woods of Upper Michigan. He wanted a simple place to hunt in the fall, a place to get away and forget all he had seen and felt in the last two years. A humble hunting camp would be his refuge when he needed an escape from the world's frustrating demands. Ethan was tired of taking orders, tired of foxholes and trenches, tired of the endless explosions ringing in his ears. His dream was to return to the U.P.'s peaceful woods and make a fresh start.

Returning home, Ethan found a job working at the Soo Lumber Mill and, before too long, had saved enough money to buy a forty-acre parcel just north of Hessel. He soon married a pretty waitress named Norma, who had waited patiently for him while he served in the war, and together they raised two sons, Jake and Jeremy. Every season, Ethan took great pride teaching his boys the art of hunting and fishing. They both loved the outdoors as much as their father and especially looked forward to deer season each mid-November. A month before opening day, they had started spending many carefree hours hiking through the crisp autumn foliage and building a deer blind near a clearing.

The hunting camp Ethan had built was near the southeast corner of his forty acres. A two-track road wound through the small spruce forest about a half mile, leading up to the cabin.

The land was hilly in places, with a narrow creek flowing through the middle of the parcel. A horseshoe-shaped ridge stretched around the perimeter and enclosed a swampy area full of dense cedar growth where the deer liked to bed down. One of only a few cabins in the area, the Powell camp was adjacent to hundreds of acres of heavily-forested state land. After many pleasurable hunting seasons, Ethan died and left the cabin to his sons. Together, the boys would carry on the Powell camp traditions that their father had taught them over the years.

Every fall, Jake and Jeremy had posted signs around the boundaries of their property that read "Private Property, No Hunting" in an attempt to ward off trespassers. There were occasional hunters who wandered onto their property, supposedly tracking a deer that had been shot. But, for the most part, hunters respected the boundaries and restricted their hunting activities to state land.

November 15, opening day of firearms deer season in Michigan, fell on a Saturday one particular year. Jake and Jeremy took it upon themselves to arrange the annual get-together at the camp, stocking the cupboards with potatoes, pancake mix and beans, and filling the cooler with ice, beer, bacon, and eggs. Their cousins came from far and wide–Iron River, Escanaba, Drummond Island, Texas, and Tennessee—to spend a week or so in the autumn woods. They came not only to hunt trophy bucks, but also for the camaraderie, the late-night poker games, and the far-fetched tall tales that tended to boil over around the fire every evening.

Early one Saturday morning, after a good breakfast, the eight hunters at the Powell camp broke into three groups. Two of the hunters took their places in the deer blind near the swamp. The other groups hiked through the woods toward state land where they had seen fresh tracks the day before.

Several inches of snow had fallen that week, and the hunters were hopeful of seeing some action in the woods. All week long, Jake had stocked the bait pile near his deer blind with carrots, discarded pumpkins, and corn cobs. He'd broken them up and scattered them loosely under a large red pine a week earlier, and the deer had been feasting on them regularly.

On the far side of the ridge, just past the swamp, Jake and Jeremy were hiking down a two-track. Wearing their hunter-orange winter jackets and tuques and carrying their deer rifles, they walked quietly as they moved through the woods. It looked like a perfect morning for opening day. The sky was a soft blue, the sun filtering through the yellow birches onto dried leaves that had stubbornly refused to fall.

Around the bend of the trail, they heard the loud crunch of human footsteps on the frozen path. They stopped to listen. Into the clearing came four individuals clad in hunter-orange. They carried no rifles, but pots and pans instead, with heavy metal spoons. When the group saw Jake and Jeremy with their deer rifles, they instantly started beating vigorously on the pans, piercing the quiet stillness of the woods.

"Hey!" Jake shouted. "What the hell are you doing? You'll scare the deer away."

"Good. That's what we mean to do," said the tall, hollow-cheeked one, stepping forward. "You people have no need to kill deer or any other animals."

"Oh, yeah?" said Jeremy. "Who put you in charge?"

The leader of the group looked Jeremy in the eye soberly and chomped on his large wad of gum in defiance. "Listen up, boys. We represent the local animal-rights group and the anti-hunting faction. This here is state land you're on, and we have every right to come here and do as we please."

They beat their pots and pans again to make their point. Jake waved his arms at them to stop.

"Why are you bothering us here?" asked Jeremy. "We all paid for our hunting licenses, and we're not disturbing you or anybody."

One of the protesters, with a bushy beard and long black hair, pushed forward. "We own these woods and streams and animal habitats just as much as you. And we want to protect them along with the animals that happen to live here. I'm sure you don't need a deer to survive, and you can probably do without another trophy head on the wall of your den."

Jake and Jeremy both shook their heads in disbelief. They wanted to get away from the pot bangers and get back to hunting. "Just leave us alone!" shouted Jake. The hunters turned away and headed down the narrow trail through the trees. The animal-rights group let them get about twenty yards ahead but followed them, beating the pans without mercy, creating as much noise and chaos as possible. This went on for half an hour, and soon, Jake and Jeremy relented and returned to their camp.

In more than twenty-five years of deer camp, the boys had never encountered anything like this. The camp was meant to be a special place for sport and relaxation, not a political theater. Jake and Jeremy had been hunting at the camp since they were young teenagers, coached by their father, Ethan, on marksmanship and the safe way to handle firearms. Ethan had passed away two years earlier, in 1990, and it was up to the boys to carry on the camp traditions.

The rustic camp had no electricity and used a large propane tank for heat and cooking. It had a fieldstone fireplace and a simple outhouse and used kerosene lamps for light in the evening. As the family grew in number over the years, the small camp was expanded to include a couple of additional bedrooms with double bunkbeds. Jake's kids, Sarah and Michael, especially loved the rustic pine bunkbeds and, along with their mother, Jessica, often spent cool summer evenings at the camp roasting marshmallows over a roaring bonfire. Friends and family had a way of showing up unexpectedly sometimes, but there was always room for them. The camp had established many deep-rooted traditions over the years, but was mainly meant to be a refuge for relaxation. Jake and Jeremy weren't looking for trouble with these protestors, but trouble had surely found them.

Later that afternoon, the cousins returned to the camp, having seen plenty of tracks but no bucks. Jake relayed stories of the animal-rights people who had followed them throughout the woods all morning, creating chaos and scaring away any possible deer.

"What business is it of theirs to come out here and raise hell?"

Jeremy stood up and cracked a can of Pabst. "Our family has been coming to camp here every November since Dad built it after the war; that's well over forty years now. It's a family tradition."

He sipped his beer while Jake cleaned and polished his rifle. "If I see those assholes here again tomorrow, I'll give them something to think about. You watch."

When the hunters woke the next morning, they found two inches of fresh-fallen snow on the ground, perfect for tracking. After a quick breakfast of coffee, eggs, and toast, the hunters headed down the trail to check the bait pile. When they arrived, the pot bangers were there waiting for them.

"You boys are awful late gettin' started this morning," said one of the orange-clad protesters. He stuffed a wad of Juicy

Fruit in his cheek and chewed it vigorously.

"Why don't you just leave us be?" Jake said. "We're not bothering any of you."

They beat their pots and pans non-stop for half a minute. "Why don't you boys just put your firearms down, go back to your cabin, and play cards or whatever you do?"

Just then, not fifty yards away, two shots were heard. The pot bangers, thinking the hunters had sighted a deer, raced off in the direction of the shots, beating their pans along the way. Jake and Jeremy looked at each other and shrugged their shoulders, relieved to finally be rid of such annoying pests. They decided to head back to the camp to regroup.

It wasn't long before a DNR officer drove up the gravel road and stopped at the Powell camp. Jake and Jeremy walked outside with their coffee to meet him.

"Morning, boys," the officer said. "Having any luck so far?"

"Not much yet, but plenty of fresh tracks."

"I just stopped by to ask you about an encounter you had this morning back in the woods with an animal-rights group. What did they say to you?" the officer asked.

"They want us to stop hunting deer," said Jeremy incredulously. "They've been beating their pots and pans like maniacs and scaring the bejesus out of every deer within two miles of here. This harassment shouldn't be legal."

"Well, gentlemen, maybe it's not the smartest thing I've ever heard of, but they have a legal right to be on state land. No, harassment's not legal; in fact, it's a misdemeanor in Michigan. But you would have to file charges against them. Why don't you just hunt on your own land for a few days? They can't set foot on it."

"I just wish they'd stay away from us," said Jake.

"By the way," the officer asked, walking back to his car, "do you boys know anything about the tires that were shot off that Bronco out on the road? The vehicle belongs to those animal rights folks."

"We heard some shots earlier, but just assumed they were from hunters. But we'll keep our eyes open, officer."

The officer drove off and, a few minutes later, their cousins showed up at the camp, laughing and joking. "We sure showed those damn pot bangers!" said one cousin. "That should put a stop to this harassment. Say, what does a set of radials go for these days?" And they laughed again. Jeremy stared at the cousins and warned them.

"We just had a visit from the DNR. You boys best keep it to yourself if you want to stay out of hot water."

That afternoon, Jake and Jeremy decided to hunt as far away from the pot bangers as possible. They hiked over the ridge on the north side of their property to the adjacent state land. With only a couple of hours of daylight remaining, the boys took their positions beneath a tall spruce tree that was within sight of a deer run.

Their patience paid off finally, and Jake shot a twelve-point buck just before dusk. It was his first buck in five years and would make a fine trophy mounted above his fireplace at home. He would take the buck to a meat processor in the Soo, who would package all the venison for his freezer. After Jake and Jeremy gutted the animal and dragged the deer carcass through the woods and back to camp, they strung it up on the buck pole outside and took pictures posing with it.

Around the dinner table that evening, the cousins all toasted Jake with their beer and laughed at the hapless animal-rights crazies who had harassed them for several days. After all their efforts, they hadn't prevented a successful hunt. Jake, Jeremy, and their cousins played cards and told stories until midnight before blowing out the kerosene lamp and crawling into their bunks.

It was a long, peaceful sleep in the Powell camp that night, under a starry sky and a moonless night. A northwest wind swirled in the pines overhead and gusted until early morning.

Just after sunrise the next morning, Jake was the first one up and started a pot of coffee on the stove. On his way to the outhouse for his morning ritual, he suddenly spied a disturbing sight. His twelve-point trophy buck hanging from the pole had been sprayed with some kind of black dye. It looked like a mutilated corpse from another world. Someone had crept quietly into camp overnight and disfigured his trophy buck. The head was so damaged it could never be mounted.

"What the hell!" he shouted. "Sonofabitch! Who did this to me?"

The other hunters heard the commotion, scrambled out of the cabin, and stared up at the butchered carcass. "You know damn well who did this. Those bastard tree-huggers, those lousy animal lovers," one of the cousins said.

"Why don't we report this to the DNR, take 'em to court, and charge 'em with harassment like the officer said?" suggested another cousin.

"No, that would be too good for them," said Jake. "They'll mention their tires being shot out, and we'll be in hot water. Let's just take care of this ourselves."

"OK," a cousin vowed, "it's payback time. We've got to chase those pricks out of these woods for good."

By the time they had cooled down, it was nearly 10 a.m.

They spruced up the cabin and climbed into their long johns, wool coats, and hunter-orange jackets. It wouldn't take long, they knew, for the pot bangers to locate the hunters in their preferred spots. Jake, Jeremy, and two of their cousins grabbed their rifles and marched down the trail toward the bait pile. They had barely crossed the ridge onto state land when the racket of banging pots and pans assaulted them. A group of five protesters approached the hunters nonchalantly.

"You guys sure don't give up easily, do you?" said Jeremy.

"So why don't you big, strong men just lay down your arms and surrender peacefully?" said a red-faced man at the front. "We don't plan to quit anytime soon."

Jake bristled and took the safety off his rifle.

"We have an absolute legal right," said Jeremy, "to put food on our table. We've paid for our hunting permits, and you're not going to stop us."

The protesters beat their pans again, and two of them blasted air-horns, like you might hear at a hockey game. The hunters stared grimly at them and were not amused.

"And we have the right to free speech," said the apparent leader of the gang. "But you don't have any right to kill poor, defenseless animals. Look at you big, macho guys stomping around the woods with your high-powered artillery and high-tech scopes. The deer don't stand a chance. You call this a sport? Give me a break."

Jeremy tried one more time to be reasonable. "Believe it or not, deer hunters do serve a worthwhile purpose. They help to thin out the herd and make it stronger. Many of these deer would starve over the winter otherwise."

"Oh, yeah? We've heard that line before, and we don't buy it."

Finally, Jake snapped. He couldn't take their arrogance and smugness anymore. "Just get the hell out of here right now!" he shouted.

Jake fired three shots directly over the protesters' heads. They were so startled they turned around and raced back down the trail toward their vehicle.

"And don't ever come back, you hear me?" Jake yelled. He fired another round over their heads for good measure. Payback, he thought, was sometimes a cruel business, but oh, so sweet. However, while Jake knew he might have scared the protesters off for a while, he also suspected he had stirred up their outrage and calls for revenge. He worried he had crossed a line he would later regret.

Late Monday afternoon, it was time to return home. The hunters packed up their gear, gathered their empties, and headed for the main road in their pickups. Jake and Jeremy were planning to return to camp the following weekend. They hoped that, by that time, the protesters would be long gone.

Two days later, the anti-hunting group showed up after dark. They wanted to make sure the Powell camp had been vacated. An empty long-necked beer bottle had been filled with gasoline and stuffed with a rag. As one of them lit the fuse with a match, he said, "This will teach those bastards not to mess with us again." And he whipped the lit bottle through a window glass. The cabin exploded in flames that soon engulfed the entire structure. By morning, nothing was left but the foundation and the stone fireplace. The protesters had disappeared without a trace.

It didn't take long for the DNR officer to figure things out. He knew the volatile situation had escalated out of control and that he should have stepped in sooner. The five protesters were arrested and charged with arson and hunter harassment. Jake was picked up and questioned by the authorities and finally charged with reckless endangerment with a firearm. He was fined and lost his hunting license for several years.

Three weeks after the cabin had burned down, Jake returned to the camp to comb through the ashes and charred remains for anything of value. In one corner where a bedroom dresser would have been, he bent over and picked up a blackened pocket watch. He rubbed the soot off on his canvas jacket and read the inscription on the silvery back: *Please come home safely. Love, Norma.* It was the pocket watch his then girlfriend had given Ethan before he'd gone off to war. As Jake held the watch in his hand, he thought of all the sacrifices his father had made and all the hard work he must have put into building the Powell camp. At that point, there was no longer any question in his mind. Jake vowed that, one way or another, he and Jeremy would rebuild the camp just the way it had been earlier. They would go back to hunting on their own land and taking care of the bait pile. It would need renewal with fresh carrots, corn cobs, and apples for the deer. It would always be part of a long-standing family tradition.

About the Author

Having lived in his native Michigan's Upper Peninsula for more than fifty years, Richard Hill has absorbed many of the colorful stories and characters that permeate this rural, isolated part of the country. He has published three books previously: *Lake Effect: A Deckhand's Journey on the Great Lakes Freighters*, *Hitchhiking After Dark: Offbeat Stories from a Small Town* (first-place winner in humor at Midwest Book Awards), and *Lost in the Woods: Building a Life Up North*. Richard attended the University of Michigan, Northern Michigan University, and the Great Lakes Maritime Academy, and currently lives near Sault Ste. Marie with his wife and cocker spaniel.